ABOUT THIS BOOK

Before there was a curse, there was a wish.

For generations, Noelani has lived in the forest of Havenwood Falls, bestowing blessings and good fortune on all who drink from the waters of her well. Over the years, she has been visited by hundreds of blushing brides and aging widows who crave her magic, but never has she met a heart as pure as that of Stella Malley—or as dark as that of her fiancé, Peter Heilen.

When the couple arrives in Havenwood Falls in the autumn of 1993, the warm waters of Noelani's well begin to run cold, and a bitter chill sets in to the naiad's heart as the forest darkens around her.

When Stella receives a postcard from the picturesque town of Havenwood Falls with an invite for Stella to sing at the Haven Saloon, the couple decides to skip the big wedding and elope. The more Stella falls in love with the town, the stranger Peter begins to act. After hearing stories of the magical, love-imbued waters of Noelani's well, Stella believes it may be the only way to save her love from his dark path and return Peter's heart to her. Little does she know that the wish she casts at the water's edge may doom them all.

LEGENDS OF HAVENWOOD
FALLS BOOKS

Also try the main Havenwood Falls series; the YA line, Havenwood Falls High; the darker, sexier side of town, Havenwood Falls Sin & Silk; and the local supernatural college, Sun & Moon Academy.

Stay up to date at www.HavenwoodFalls.com

BOOKS BY SEVEN JANE

The Isle of Gold

A Midnight Clear

Of Salt and Stars (Havenwood Falls)

The Drowning Bride (Legends of Havenwood Falls)

Havenwood Falls Short Story Anthology 2019

THE DROWNING BRIDE

SEVEN JANE

For my part, I know nothing with any certainty, but the sight of the stars makes me dream.
—Vincent van Gogh

In loving memory of BB.

CHAPTER 1

$\mathcal{T}$he fall of 1993 was a particularly lovely one, even in Pensacola, where autumn didn't normally show its colors, much less announce itself with the usual splendor that it did in other parts of the eastern United States. With an average two hundred and twenty-four sunny days per year, northern Florida was a year-round blue-sky paradise, with temperatures that rarely dipped below ninety before late September and sometimes not even then.

It almost never got cold enough for a real coat, and you could forget about winter, which might have gone by completely unnoticed were it not for the holiday season that inspired people to deck palm trees with Christmas lights and play "Mele Kalikimaka" on every local radio station. In Florida, Santa wore swimming trunks and Ray-Bans when he came for his annual deliveries—and why not? This part of the country hadn't seen enough snow to turn anything fully white since the late seventies, and even then it only very barely qualified as a dusting—at least by New York standards, Stella's home state.

Now, in mid-September, other than a slight crisp in the evening breeze and a few blushing dogwood trees, it was nearly impossible to tell that the fall equinox was only a few days away, and Stella Malley was trying to come to terms with the fact that this would be the first time she'd celebrate the coming of fall in a place that almost never bothered itself to be anything other than summer.

The thought cooled her in the way that a crisp autumn breeze would have, even if it did smell like saltwater.

"It's a hundred degrees outside and not a sign of fall in sight, and I'm still chilly," Stella grumbled to herself, brushing the palms of her hands down her forearms and wishing she'd had the forethought to keep a light jacket in her car, even though people would have teased her for doing so. She slid behind the wheel and cranked the engine to life, ready to drive home in the dark after work, alone with her radio and her thoughts. Music blared reliably from the speakers, but true enough, it was after midnight and the thermometer on the bank she passed still read 89 degrees—not a temperature that fell within her idyllic fall range.

Stella turned her mind toward happier things and tried to think cooler thoughts, but at the moment such a thing was a tall order, even for Stella, who was nothing if not a perpetual optimist.

It wasn't simply the lack of fall foliage that put a damper on her usually high spirits. Stella was already feeling seasonally out of place, and winter, she knew, was going to be truly bizarre by the time December came around. She'd be lying if she said she wasn't excited to spend the holidays buried in white sand rather than in the snow she'd grown up with in upstate New York, but still, despite how long she had dreamed of living on the beach and how happy she was to call Florida her new home with her fiancé Peter, Stella was still a little anxious about her first holidays in the Sunshine State. A deep aching had settled into her bones during the last days of August, when holiday decorations had begun appearing on the shelves in the department stores around town. She and Peter had moved halfway across the country over the summer, right after May Day. As a result, this would be the first year she wouldn't be able to partake in her family's seasonal celebrations.

Stella considered herself an independent, modern woman, but still she yearned for tradition and family, something she was moving toward but hadn't quite reached yet with Peter. She might have been twenty-two and ready to settle down and start her own life, but that didn't make the uprooting any easier, not even when she'd spent her whole life wishing she were somewhere warmer. Her mother was Nigerian by way of Haiti, and had inspired Stella with stories of sunshine and tropical climates, but her father was of Irish descent, and among the many mixed ethnic traditions celebrated in her childhood home, the spring and fall equinoxes had been her favorites. Her dad had called the fall equinox Mabon, a celebration that honored a moment of harvest, when the Welsh god Mabon performed his act of pure love with the cutting of the last grain and died until his return in spring.

"Fall is a season of balance," her dad had been fond of saying, his freckles lit up like fireflies with excitement as he taught Stella how to plait a sheaf of corn into a dolly. "This is the time of year that you reap what you sow, a harvest before we return to the darkness from whence we came to await the rebirth of the new year."

Her mother would scoff; her beloved Port-au-Prince was just as hot and humid this time of year as Florida, and she had never fully bought into seasonal change. But Stella had always liked her father's version best—that fall was the cusp of transition, when the old faded away so that something new could grow in its place.

That was another reason this year's fall season seemed even more special, and even sadder to miss celebrating in full: right now Stella was just a girl in love. Come spring, she would be a bride, and together she and Peter would begin their new life as husband and wife here in Pensacola, where spring and summer and fall and winter all melded into one season of sand and sea.

Thinking of it that way, Stella couldn't help but fancy herself as the god Mabon himself: prepared to perform an act of pure love and await the spring. She was giving up changing leaves and cooler weather for the greater good—for her future and for her fiancé—and come spring, it would all be worth it. Who cared about the weather when you carried the spirit of the season in your heart?

This year, she resolved, even if she couldn't see it in the balmy, perpetually summer weather outside or celebrate it in the usual ways, Stella could still feel fall in her bones. That, she figured, like the transformation that came along when the sun headed south over the celestial equator, was what was making her restless—unbalanced. All five foot nine of her wasn't just a woman at all, but a leaf, ready to transform her colors from bright summer green to crimson or gold or even deep, earthy burgundy. She was in the final stages of harvest and ready to be reborn—in a new place, with a new family and a new name.

Having found a way to knit together her worries and anxieties and turn the half-empty glass back to half-full status, Stella hummed along on her ride home, thinking cooler thoughts after all. She wasn't just a girl away from home and lamenting seasons lost, but a woman on the verge of becoming something new. She was preparing for the harvest of all she'd worked for in reaching both for her dreams and her future.

Now, she could feel it. The feeling of fall was a crisp breath on her wheatish skin and the sound of rustling, dry leaves in her ears. It was the warm scent of pumpkins and cinnamon blooming from the air freshener she'd picked up tonight at the Kmart on Highway 90 and hung from the rearview mirror of her Ford Probe that was the same powder blue as the sky at dawn. Stella flicked the little cardboard tree and twisted the volume knob on her radio up another notch, her voice rising to match as she sped toward home through the late-night darkness of near-midnight.

Elsewhere, deep in a forest edged by mountains, a single, crimson leaf fell from a branch above. It floated downward, wafting to and fro, and alighted on the surface of still water in a stone well, where a woman picked it up with interest and held it up in front of her face. She watched as the tender edges of the leaf began to frost and curl with cold, and then she shivered and cast the leaf away from her well.

Noelani, the Lady of the Water, slipped her toes back into the water and thought about love as a pair of young women, their arms laden with wildflowers, made their way under the moonlight to ask her blessing.

$\sim$

Stella's coupe had been an early wedding present from her soon-to-be husband, Peter Heilen.

It was her dream car—brand new, sleek and sporty, and Peter hadn't approved of the car any more than he'd approved of Stella adding the underbody lights or installing the subwoofer in the hatchback. He'd said it was overkill; that such behavior put her in the spotlight—the kind that would make men with bad intentions take notice of her when she was alone in the dark. But this didn't bother Stella one bit. With him beside her, she argued, what harm could possibly come to her? Besides, she loved to be in the light, particularly if she was the star shining in its center.

Peter knew that, too, and while he didn't particularly approve of it either, it was what Stella thought he loved her for most, even if he pretended otherwise.

"Do you really have to blare Mariah Carey at full volume every time you get in your car?" was a question he had asked on more than one occasion. Sometimes it was slightly modified to "every time you go to the beach" or "every time we run to Blockbuster," but no matter how he dressed up the question, Stella's answer was always the same.

"Absolutely, yes, I do," she'd say. "Mariah is a musical goddess, just like I'm going to be one day. And that's why you love me so much, remember?" She'd follow this with her best impression of the songstress's trademark high-pitched squeal and then warble off snippets of "Dreamlover," her favorite track off Maria's new album, *Music Box*. The album held a special place in Stella's heart, since Peter had hidden her engagement ring in a beautiful blue, heart-shaped music box the night he'd proposed. She'd then punctuate the lyrics with kisses until he caved, which he always did. Stella thought Peter terribly cute when he pouted. She knew how to get her groom-to-be to turn his smile upside down, and so no matter how grumpy he got about her singing or her loud music, Stella knew that all it took were a few kisses and a little light teasing to bring Peter around.

He played at being all dark and broody, but she knew he had a soft spot in him too. She also knew that it was reserved especially for her.

"Stop," he'd protest, his not-so-earnest deflections weakening each time her lips brushed against his skin until his arms were wrapped around her and he was kissing her back, nibbling on her bottom lip as his fingers dug into the flesh below her shoulder blades. "You're such a handful," he'd tease her, calling her his little sea siren and tugging at her perpetually windblown hair that snarled her natural curls into tight balls of tangles. Stella would laugh and respond back, trying not to sound breathless with all his warm heat washing over her so she could get out the words "but you love me," at which he would groan playfully and admit, "I do, I do."

"You have the voice of an angel," he'd tell her, "even better than Mariah. It lights up the shadowy places of my soul."

Those words made Stella blush every time she heard them. She knew she wasn't anywhere near as talented as her favorite singer, but like Mariah, Stella thought that she was indeed one of those women who was born to sing. Her parents had instilled a love of song in her growing up, and Stella had parlayed that into early careers in school choirs and talent shows. She'd been captivated by the vocal talents of the women whose voices spun like magic out of her mother's big sound system that took up an entire corner of their living room— women like Whitney Houston, Chaka Khan, Paula Abdul, and Janet Jackson, strong and powerful black women with voices more beautiful than any instrument. When Mariah Carey—who had also grown up in a mixed-race home in New York—arrived on the scene in 1990, she had instantly become both Stella's muse and her inspiration.

Like Mariah, Stella had that same kind of undeniable exotic beauty that everyone always agreed was beautiful without ever worrying over why. Perhaps it was because of the rolling gingerbread curls that fell midway down her back, or her large almond-shaped eyes that were precisely the same shade of burnt amber as fossilized tree sap. Or perhaps it was her tawny complexion, the perfect blend of her mother's ebony skin and full, shapely lips, and her father's pale, freckled flesh and angular features. Whatever it was, Stella had always felt too pale for her mother's people and too dark for her father's, a part of two worlds and yet belonging to neither, and despite her inborn talent, she'd always held back from putting herself out there as a real singer. She loved the spotlight, but sometimes found it too exposing. But watching Mariah sweep the Billboards, Stella finally felt not only beautiful for the first time, but like she could really be something other than a girl from Rochester who sang in her shower.

The first time Stella heard "Can't Let Go" from the *Emotions* album, she decided she couldn't let go of her dream to sing. She styled herself after her favorite musical idol, right down to the cropped denim shorts and knotted flannel shirt, and got her first real gig singing weeknights at a hole in the wall called the Skylark, which was a little less Cheers and a lot more Bar Fly than she would have preferred—but it was a start.

Sometimes all it took for something magical to happen was a little spark to start the fire.

It had been her voice that had led Stella and Peter to meet in the first place, too. One night after her set, right as the bar was closing down, a tall man with dishwater blond hair and piercing green eyes had come up and introduced himself. Stella's mother had warned her never to date a man she met in the bar where she worked, but he'd been charming, so she'd agreed to share a drink with him the following night. Three weeks later, Stella and Peter were engaged. They left New York the following summer. Her parents hadn't been too happy about it, but then Stella supposed most parents probably weren't happy when their children grew up, fell in love with a stranger, and moved a thousand miles away from home.

"You barely know him, Stella," her mother had admonished, making the sign of the cross over her chest, the way she always did when she worried about evil spirits or people with bad intentions. "No good can come from running away with a man you barely know."

"You barely knew me, Rachelle," Stella's father, Kieran, had countered. He ignored the clicking rattlesnake sound his wife made with her tongue when she was getting angry. What he'd said next had been enough to avoid Stella's mother's wrath and maybe even make her agree, though she would never have admitted it. "Follow your heart and your dreams," he advised. "Sometimes they lead to the same place. It might not be what you expect, but it'll get you there."

So far, they had, even though the path had been a little bumpier than she might have preferred. Stella and Peter were polar opposites in nearly every way, from food choices to fashion sense, but the couple was as madly in love almost a year after their engagement as they'd been on that first night in the lounge, and falling further every day. Peter wasn't really being critical when he complained about her music, and Stella knew that too. And his gloomy mood had nothing to do with the volume of her radio or the undercarriage lights on her car, or even how much hot water she wasted rehearsing her sets in the shower.

He'd been a little temperamental since they'd moved down near the beach. Peter preferred the tranquility of mountains and forests to the hot sun and the noisy rush of the waves breaking upon the shore, while Stella, naturally, felt the exact opposite. Mountains made her feel boxed in; they were so big and tall and overwhelming that she worried she might suffocate in their presence. In Stella's mind, the sounds of the ocean were just another form of music— the cry of gulls, the rush of waves, the sough of wind over the water —but Peter said being so near to the ocean made him feel on edge, like all those lovely noises were mocking him and he was going to be sucked out to sea and fall off the edge of the earth or something. He complained when the beach sand followed them into the house and bemoaned the constant application of sunscreen, but in spite of how much he claimed he disliked the beach, when Stella had been offered the singing gig at the jazz lounge in the heart of Pensacola Beach Boardwalk, she'd been prepared to turn it down until Peter had said his landscape preferences weren't worth her giving up her dreams.

So they'd gone.

And so it didn't matter that Peter was a habitual grump. Stella was calm and even-tempered with her lovable curmudgeon, and since her love had given up his mountains to take her to the sea, it was easy for her to be patient with Peter—and extra careful to keep the sand out of his side of the bed.

That was, after all, what Mabon had been all about, right? Sacrifice and pure love. And so no matter how dark it got—whether it was the waning, autumn-less end of year or Peter's moods—there was always light just ahead.

And Stella would be Peter's beacon, both on stage and off. She would rescue him from his darkness and bring him back into the light with her. Maybe then he'd learn to see the same beauty in the water that she did.

CHAPTER 2

*S*itting on the back porch and thinking about how much he wished the whole damn ocean would freeze over, Peter heard Stella's car long before its wheels crunched up the sandy shell driveway of their rented beach house on Sandpiper Lane. Peter always sensed Stella coming when she made her way toward him, with a sort of tinnitus-like sound that was even shriller than his inner musings on how unsettled being so near to the open ocean made him feel—which was saying something, because he hated being so close to the water.

It made him feel exposed and gave him the uncomfortable sensation that something was watching him—waiting for him—and yet still he sat on the porch and glared at the waves, almost as if he were daring whatever watched him to come for him.

Peter, the water seemed to call as the waves broke upon the shore. *Peter, come to us.*

With a sigh, Peter set down the empty bottle of beer he'd been holding next to another empty bottle on the small outdoor table, and moved back inside the ugly little beach house. The landlord—a middle aged man with a feather earring and a seemingly endless supply of Hammer pants—had painted the small two-story building the rosy, optimistic color of a living conch shell, but with its spindly staircase and squat, layered frame, the house reminded Peter more of a petulant crab that had washed up on shore than a shell.

The house was ramshackle and could use a good bit of maintenance, but even with its current state of disrepair it was some sort of paradise to his fiancée, who refused to move to a more sensible apartment closer to the heart of town. No matter how much Peter tried to convince her that this place was less a paradise and much more likely to be in danger of being swept out to sea during a hurricane—a real and frequent threat in the Gulf, particularly during this part of this year—Stella wouldn't hear it. But then, he and Stella rarely ever agreed on much when it came to beach life, so that was to be expected.

"This place is a disaster waiting to happen," Peter had professed when she'd first shown him the unit for rent.

She'd laughed and responded with, "Don't be silly, Pete. It just has character."

He'd thought character looked a lot like disaster, but he'd signed the lease anyway. Anything to keep Stella happy.

That had been the normal course of life since he'd met her— Peter and Stella rarely agreed on much of anything, but this only had the odd quirk of making him love her even more. He was drawn to Stella like a moth to a flame, or the negative end of a magnet to her positive, or whatever other cliché saying made sense to describe the incredible power of attraction he felt to Stella despite the total polarities at which they existed. Stella was the only woman on earth who could drive Peter so often to the brink of madness while at the same time having the singular ability to allow him to feel such deep feelings of love and devotion that he had never felt about any other person before.

He loved her—for better or worse, he loved her with his entire heart.

Peter watched through the living room curtains as Stella's sporty blue coupe pulled into the drive and came to a stop. He waited for her to exit the car, his thoughts moving away from the water and the ugly little beach house and to his beautiful bride-to-be.

Even though she insisted on blaring her music at unreasonable volumes day or night, the sound of her booming stereo wasn't how Peter knew Stella was almost home, and the sound of her arrival didn't stop once her engine had cut off and the stereo gone silent. That was something . . . else. It was difficult to articulate it, and he'd never even attempted to describe it to another living soul—both because he couldn't and because to try would probably make him sound insane—but he could sense the woman's presence. It called him to her, and it had been what pulled him off the road in Rochester and drew him to that grimy little dive bar, the Skylark, effectively ending his plans to head up to Canada. He'd been on his way to Acadia, intent on losing himself in the forests and mountains that insulated him from the coast and abandoning himself to solitude for a while.

Peter had always considered himself a pretty average, decent guy, but something had changed in him around the time he hit twenty, and he didn't like the man he felt like he was becoming. He felt unsettled, antsy, and a depressive cloud had descended on him—and then there had been the accident.

Laura, Peter's ex-girlfriend, had drowned early the summer before, when the two of them had been on a camping trip down in Shenandoah National Park. Peter had never been able to fully understand what had happened that day. One minute, Laura was in the canoe with him, her bright auburn hair whipping around her head in the wind while she laughed and splashed him with water from her oar. The next, she was gone and he was soaking wet, clinging to the hull of the upturned canoe. As for what had happened between, Peter wasn't sure what was real or what had been filled into his memory in the series of nightmares he'd endured afterward. The rangers had found Laura's body floating on the other side of the lake. After a fruitless investigation, it had been assumed that something had capsized the small boat—maybe they'd been moving around too much, having too much of a good time splashing each other, and flipped. Peter must have been knocked out, maybe hit his head on the fiberglass siding and come to in time to fling himself back across the bobbing boat, but Laura must have remained underwater. She'd drowned and Peter had lived, but he couldn't help thinking that, somehow, he was to blame for what happened out on the lake.

No, he'd known he was. He just didn't want to admit it.

Peter, Laura's voice still sometimes called in the whisper of waves breaking on the sand—just another reason Peter hated the beach. In his dreams, he saw her face staring at him from beneath the water.

So Peter had fled, trying to get as far away from himself and that memory as possible, but his mood only seemed to worsen the farther he traveled up the eastern seaboard. Glimpses of coast constantly winked in and out of view along that drive, making it impossible for him to wrestle his thoughts away from the day at the lake. By the time he'd reached Rochester, Peter was already dreading crossing the bridge over Niagara into Buffalo, but then out of nowhere a weird feeling had come over him, calling like a siren to a sailor over water. It had possessed him to get off the highway and take up two parking spots at the Skylark.

The first thing his eyes had landed on when he stumbled into that dimly lit little dump was the source of the song itself, crooning her heart out up on a makeshift stage: Stella Malley.

From the first moment he saw Stella, Peter was smitten. Everything about her smoldered, from her amber eyes down to the long, long length of a pair of legs that looked every bit as strong and graceful as the tall pines he had loved to climb as a boy. He took one look at Stella and fell irretrievably into her gravitational pull, orbiting her from that moment forth as surely as a moon circles a heavenly body. He'd sat at a small, wobbling table in the back of the room and listened to her sing, knowing she was destined to be a star and just as surely knowing he'd follow her anywhere, which was at once both liberating and troubling.

He was a goner; she had him hook, line, and sinker—whether he liked it or not. He'd waited out her set and then approached the stage. She'd seemed shy but warm when she shook his hand, but he could tell she resisted, so Peter pleaded and did his best to charm her until she finally agreed to meet him for drinks the following night. He counted every single minute for the next twenty or so hours until their meeting time, and still couldn't believe it when she actually showed up, wearing a bright pink cocktail dress with little rhinestone buttons on the straps that made her eyes shimmer.

He'd bought the best diamond ring he could afford the very next day and kept it in a little glass music box in the glove compartment of his car. Whatever plans he had of taking the murky madness banging around inside his head to the Canadian forest were over. He might not know exactly who he was yet, but he knew he never wanted to be free of Stella Malley. As maddening as it was, marrying her was now the only thing he wanted to do.

Peter hadn't been happy about moving to Florida, much less setting up residence so close to the water that he could literally step into the surf if he wasn't careful, but having Stella come home to him every night made it worth it. Besides, as a freelance travel writer he could work from anywhere, and pieces about the beach sold as well as any, maybe even better. Everyone—everyone other than him, anyway—seemed to love being on the water.

That's what Peter thought of now as he watched Stella fuss with her hair in the driver's side mirror, trying to smooth down unruly curls that had been tangled into a frenzy from driving with the windows down. He laughed under his breath, admiring the view as Stella extracted herself from her car, barefoot and carrying her heels. She left every night dressed to the nines to sing at the club. Tonight, she wore a sleek red number with skinny satin straps that accentuated every single one of her beautiful curves and made Peter's skin flush with both desire and jealousy of what other men in the club might have thought while they watched his bride perform this evening.

The thought made Peter cringe, and the taste of envy soured his tongue. She was his.

Peter, the ghost of girlfriends past called. He ignored it.

Stella's curls were disheveled, and one of her dress straps had come loose over her shoulder, but to Peter she was the most gorgeous creature he had ever seen. He couldn't wait to take her in his arms.

Stella spotted him watching out the front window and smiled, waving so that the shoes in her hand banged against each other like the world's most awkward wind chimes. Peter smiled back and met her at the front door.

"You heard me coming again, huh?" She smiled, biting her lower lip in that way she did when she thought he might fuss. He didn't think she realized she even did it, which made him love it even more. Then again, he also didn't think he fussed.

"All the way up the road," he taunted, "maybe even the moment you got in the car after work. What was that tonight? Toni Braxton?"

"Janet," Stella corrected, naming both the artist—the "princess of America's black royal family," as quoted in *Rolling Stone*—and the album's title in one word. Janet, like Mariah or Madonna, didn't need a last name, according to Stella. Their first must have been powerful enough, he figured.

Nevertheless, Peter provided it, adding his own twist. "Ah, Ms. Jackson, then." He looped one arm around Stella and pulled her in for a quick kiss. "How about Mrs. Heilen?"

Stella snickered and wriggled free of his grasp, then tossed her shoes into the already huge pile at the door and began making her way to examine the stack of unopened mail on the counter. Peter tried not to wince. She was beautiful, his songbird, but not neat. If it were up to Stella, the whole house might become one giant unkempt closet and every dish in the kitchen would get used before a single one found its way back into the cabinet.

"If you're nasty," she shot back over her shoulder, completing the song lyric as she bit her lip again, and Peter instantly stopped caring about Stella's lack of domestic prowess. The urge to wrap her in his arms increased. He wanted to wrap himself around her, hold her as tight as he could.

"How about if I just ask really, really nicely?" Peter negotiated as he sidled up behind her. He rested his chin atop her head, breathing in her sweet, smoky scent and waiting for a response while she rifled through stacks of bills and junk mail. Stella was sorting the mail into two piles, those that Peter liked to think of as "junk mail Stella will scatter around the house for months and inevitably throw away" and "bills she'll plan to pay but will then promptly forget until the past due notice comes." Of course, he wouldn't tell her that. He'd just go through it again later and tidy up behind her.

Clutching—rumpling—a stack of mail in her hands, Stella spun on him, wedging herself between the counter and Peter in a way that pressed her body against his and made him stifle a moan. There was a mischievous glint in Stella's eyes that meant she was in a teasing mood, and her lips were curled in a devilish smirk that said very plainly that he would be the thing she'd be teasing. She must have had a great night at work. The sharp prick of jealousy flared again in the back of Peter's mind as he thought about how sexy Stella looked on stage. Instantly, he decided he'd go to work with her the following night and watch her sing. He hadn't done so in weeks.

"Really nicely," Stella repeated, stretching out the word in a singsong tune that sounded a whole lot less nice and a lot more naughty. She lifted her lips to his and that little ringing Stella soundtrack that always played when she was near reverberated through Peter's head.

It was loud, suddenly, too loud, and punctuated by a weird sound of rushing water, like a faucet turned on too high. Peter kissed her quickly so she wouldn't think something was wrong, then backed away to a safe distance. He must have had more to drink than he'd realized—two beers, maybe three, or had it been more? His insides were twisted. It felt like half of him wanted to kiss Stella and the other half wanted to . . . he didn't want to say, even in his own mind. The memory of Laura's auburn hair whipping in the wind flashed through Peter's thoughts, and he shook it out of his mind. The faucet ruckus decreased until it was just the sound of Stella still shuffling through mail.

It had to be the water, Peter thought. He shouldn't have sat outside and toyed with it. His nerves were fraying. Maybe they could take a trip up to Georgia or maybe over to Alabama, get lost in the woods for a little bit and away from the damned beach. There were deciduous trees there, and the temperatures would be cooler, too. Stella would get her fix of fall. It'd be a win-win.

"How was work?" he asked, desperate to move on to happier—drier—subjects.

"Oh, you know," she muttered dismissively, oblivious to Peter's inner turmoil as she flipped the pages of a clothing catalog. "Same old. I sing, they clap, and then everybody gets bored and the drinks dry up. It gets late, and they all go home. I need a change of scenery, just for a night or two. Maybe I can audition to sing at that place over the bridge, in Mobile."

Peter cleared his throat, ready to grasp the opportunity that had magically offered itself up before him. "You sound upset," he goaded, hoping she'd say she was. "Do you not like it here?"

Stella was more open to change—and more impulsive—when she was unhappy. Maybe he could finagle his way into more than a trip; maybe he could talk her into moving away from this stupid beachy hellhole.

A change of scenery could be good for both of them. He still wasn't sure why he'd agreed to Florida in the first place.

Stella looked at him for the first time since she'd started examining the mail, and her eyes were thoughtful, free of teasing. "Not upset, but maybe a little . . . I don't know . . . tired," she admitted. "I think it's the season, or rather, the lack thereof. It feels like home here every other day but today, no matter how I try to reason it out in my head. I love Pensacola, but I do miss the cooler weather and the colorful leaves. It's just not fall without that, you know?"

Oh, do I ever, Peter thought. This was not the first time Stella had complained about missing fall. He could agree on that point. The only color Peter ever saw here was his least favorite: blue.

"Maybe we should start thinking about our honeymoon," Stella suggested, her voice light around the edges. "We could look into going up to the mountains or something. Maybe the Poconos? I've heard about a resort there that's just for honeymooners."

"Our wedding isn't until spring," Peter reminded her, trying to keep on the subject of right now rather than derailing into wedding planning. He was a guy, after all, and could only tolerate so much talk about gowns and flowers and cakes. "That's a long way away, and definitely after fall. I don't want you to be unhappy all winter."

Stella countered. "I know, but this place I'm thinking of isn't just a fall resort. There's tons to do in the spring and summer, too— hiking, horseback riding, canoeing." Peter cringed, glad he'd never told Stella about the accident on the lake. "Oh! There's even spas in every bridal suite, and they're, like, shaped like martini glasses, so you have to climb a little ladder to get in. How diva is that?"

Peter knew exactly what resort Stella was talking about—Cove Haven—he'd found a brochure stuffed inside one of her bridal magazines in the bathroom. It sounded kitschy and overpriced, but there was one thing attractive about it: it was in the mountains. Peter was just about to agree, thinking that the Pocono Mountains in Pennsylvania weren't far from New York, and if he could just stick it out through winter, then maybe once they were married and already so far away from the beach, he could wheedle his way into convincing Stella that the city would be a cornucopia of opportunity for a budding songstress, when her voice—eager this time—interrupted his thoughts.

"Oh my gosh, Pete, did you see this?" She waved an oversized glossy postcard from the bottom of the mail pile in his direction. Her eyes scanned it again, and then she did that little bouncing thing that all girls seemed to do when they were excited about something. "It's an invitation to some place called the Haven Saloon in Colorado. They've invited me to come and sing as a special guest!"

Well, this was just too good to be true, Peter thought—like the invite had arrived by magic.

"Where in Colorado?" he asked. Colorado was nice and landlocked. Perfect.

"Someplace called Havenwood Falls." Stella shrugged and passed the postcard to him. "I've never heard of it. Do you think it's real, or one of those scammy junk mail things? Like I'll get there and have to pay to sing or something?"

"I think it's fate," Peter said, examining the postcard. On the front was a view of sweeping, snow-topped mountains surrounded by dense forest of bushy evergreens and vibrant, fall-flowering trees. Nestled in the heart of a box canyon was what looked like a quiet little town, the kind beloved by tourists and rich people who had spare homes to go with the seasons. On the back, just like Stella had said, was a short message written in smooth cursive:

Dear Stella Malley,

If you're up for a trip to Colorado, we'd love to have you at the Haven Saloon. We think you'll find our peaceful little town a magical place to share your voice. We have room here just for you.

Too good to be true or not, that was all it took for the perfect plan to arrive in Peter's mind. He wanted mountains and serenity, Stella wanted to sing, and both of them were tired of waiting for their wedding day. Peter took one look out the window, at the waves slapping around under the moonlight, and tossed the postcard on the counter. He swept Stella up in his arms, swinging her from side to side in time with the tingling in his ears, and for the first time since they'd moved to the beach, loving the musical sound of his little songbird's call.

"Pack your bags and tell your boss you're taking the next couple of days off," he told her between kisses. "I'm ready to marry you, my little sea siren, and we're eloping to Havenwood Falls."

CHAPTER 3

*E*loping wasn't something Stella ever thought she would do. Ever since she was a little girl, she'd dreamed of having the big, traditional wedding—the white dress, the tiara, the crystal champagne flutes—all the trimmings that would make her feel like a princess on her big day. She'd had visions of walking down the aisle with her father and serenading the man waiting for her at the altar—the man who would be her husband at the very moment she said "I do." An iconic love ballad would play during her vows. Whitney Houston's rendition of "I Will Always Love You" had been at the top of that list, or better yet, Etta James's "At Last."

She'd built dream boards and collages of weddings, scrapped together with magazine pictures as she assembled the Perfect Wedding Day. When she and Peter had gotten engaged, Stella immediately started thinking about things like where to set up her wedding registry and making bridal fitting appointments for her and her eleven closest girlfriends, all of whom she planned to dress in pale shades of lavender. But the move to Pensacola had thrown a kink in wedding planning, and she'd had to rethink everything from the flowers to the venue.

The truth was, she hadn't made much progress on the actual plan itself so much as she had on daydreaming about making the plan. When Peter suggested they take advantage of the mysterious invitation and elope to the unknown town of Havenwood Falls somewhere in Colorado, though it was apparently too small to be mentioned on any map, it was hard to say no—and not just because it was her first real invite to sing or because there would be actual fall in Colorado.

Stella knew that a big fancy wedding, regardless of where it happened or how many attendants they had in the bridal party—a number that, despite her protests, Peter had already whittled down to no more than two apiece, and even that had been a hard-fought victory—was not what her beloved truly wanted. And, she decided, it was something she could live without if it meant Peter's happiness. Mabon, she reminded herself. Sacrifice.

And so Stella packed a suitcase, making sure to include both her best performance dress and the glass music box that had once contained her engagement ring but now held both of their wedding bands, and boarded a flight to Denver International Airport with the hopes of making a stellar debut at the Haven Saloon before getting married under the brilliant canvas of autumn treetops she'd been longing for. She didn't need the big, fancy wedding with the dress and tiara and crystal. All she really needed was a place to sing her vows to the man of her dreams, and if she could do it somewhere beautiful with real falling leaves, then right now there was nothing else she wanted more.

Maybe an autumn equinox wedding was just what all her craving for fall had been leading her toward anyway. It was change. A new season. An opportunity for her and Peter to put away their old lives and spend winter cocooning for the spring of the future.

Either that or she was just being selfish, and this would all be for nothing. Stella had the odd feeling that the invite to the Haven Saloon had been a solo one—"We have room here just for you"—and not a couples invite, but there was no way she was leaving Peter behind, so she hadn't even given voice to that thought.

Now, sitting beside her, even with his brow furrowed in confusion as he scoured the state map of Colorado, hunting for the telltale dot that would identify Havenwood Falls somewhere between Grand Junction and Durango, Stella could see relaxation had already softened the rough edges of Peter's expression. His sharp green eyes had mellowed to the color of jade, and she could see the dimples in his cheeks now that he'd stopped clenching his jaw. It had been a while since he'd looked so at peace.

Maybe moving out to the beach had been a bad idea after all. Stella loved it, but Peter's hatred for living on the water seemed to be more than a landscape preference. They would both have to learn to compromise and communicate better—that was the bedrock of relationships that lasted, wasn't it?

"You're sure this is the area it's in?" Peter asked for what must have been the hundredth time that morning. He was holding the map closer to his eyes now, like he might be able to make out a teensy, tiny dot if the paper were close enough to his face.

"I'm sure. The guy I talked to at the Haven Saloon said the closest town we'd probably see on the map is Grand Junction, which is about a two-hour drive north. Montrose is closer, but it's smaller," she said, visualizing the space in her mind. "Durango is south." Stella repeated this easily, quoting the directions the saloon's owner, a laid-back dude who'd introduced himself as Brent, had given her over the phone. Stella didn't mention that Brent didn't seem to have any recollection of sending her the postcard or inviting her to sing at his saloon, but he'd covered this up with a laugh that sounded like he'd been spending some time with Mary Jane, and said that things worked a little differently sometimes in Havenwood Falls.

If she'd gotten an invite to sing, well, then she was welcome to come on down and sing.

"I just don't know why it's not on the map. It's like it doesn't exist," Peter mumbled, mostly to himself. "Weird."

The captain announced their final descent, and Peter folded the map he'd picked up in the airport convenience store, then tucked it into the seat pocket in front of him. Stella braced herself for another round of questions about the location of a town not found on any map, but instead Peter leaned his head back on the headrest and sighed contentedly. Even though eloping was his idea, Peter had been unsatisfied with the amount of information he'd been able to find on the town. It hadn't been much. Mostly what Stella had discovered when she'd phoned the few places referred by other places to set up their trip in a sort of telephone tag—a place called Whisper Falls Inn, where she had booked a room for their stay, and the local courthouse, where they'd be able to pick up a marriage license. Peter, who liked to plan everything down to the nitty gritty details, had mercifully stepped aside to let Stella plan the trip, and though she was completely out of her element, Stella thought the spontaneous trip to the mysterious town was the height of good fun.

Peter's hand found Stella's and gave it a quick squeeze. He lifted her knuckles to his lips.

"At least if there's a shuttle, we don't have to know where it is, right, babe? We just look for the bus stop, wait for it to show up, and climb aboard. Did you ever find out how often the shuttle runs?"

Stella sucked her teeth, anticipating a rebuttal. "No, I didn't. I forgot. Sorry."

"Well, if it's the preferred way into town, it must be pretty often, right?"

"Right," she agreed, stifling a yawn. Brent hadn't said what time the shuttle ran, but he had said the ride into Havenwood Falls from the Denver airport was a good five- or six-hour drive, depending on road conditions. The complimentary shuttle would take them the entire way, no problem, but she'd totally spaced on asking what time it actually showed up. Hopefully it wouldn't be a long wait. Peter had booked the first flight of the morning out of Pensacola, and between the early flight and the time difference, Stella was looking forward to taking a nap on the long drive up into the mountains. If all went well, they'd arrive in town sometime in the early afternoon, which was just enough time to check into the inn, get a quick bite to eat somewhere local, and show up nice and refreshed at the Haven Saloon for her inaugural performance.

Peter nuzzled against Stella's ear as the plane's wheels touched down in Denver. "I can't wait to get my arms around you in this secret little town," he teased, his voice purring darkly against her skin. "This trip is going to change everything, babe. Just wait and see. This gig in Havenwood Falls is just the beginning. It's all up from here. Once you sing one night, no one will ever forget your name. You'll be a legend."

~

A few hundred miles away in Havenwood Falls, Noelani shivered.

Ever since the first leaf fell the day before, she had noticed the fall that bloomed in the trees surrounding her meadow in the forest seemed chillier than usual. The wildflowers kept their petals closed even at noon, and the water of her well—which no matter what season or time of day always stayed as warm as if the sun still shone brightly upon it—had begun to grow icy. Goose bumps prickled along her skin, and frost had begun to form in the lengths of her hair and spiderweb along the stones of her well when she sat atop its brim. But it wasn't just the outside that had begun to change; her heart, too, seemed to be freezing inside her chest.

She felt weak and vaguely ill, as if the magic inside her had begun to fade away.

"Are you all right, my lady?" a young girl's voice spoke over her ear as Noelani sat, swirling her finger idly in the water and wondering what had caused her well to run cold. It was a difficult task, for naiads had very little sense of time and rarely concerned themselves with things that did not directly affect them, which was nearly all things.

Noelani closed her eyes and shook her head without turning. She hadn't sensed the girl approach, and even on her best days didn't allow just anyone to catch more than a glimpse of her before she disappeared beneath the waters of her well. It was unwise, particularly when she did not know well the heart whose eyes looked upon her. Her water she would give freely; she never turned away a wish for love made in good faith and gave her blessings to humans and supernatural creatures alike, to the town's residents and visitors, men and women who loved other men and women regardless of the conventions of the times. But for someone to see her would mean that some of her magic would stay with them, tucked safely inside the memory of that sight, to be carried in their hearts for the rest of their days. For that kind of blessing, she had to be sure the desire for love was pure. Otherwise, even her magic would sour and turn dark within them, and she would share the blame in whatever evil it did.

"Yes, sweetheart," answered Noelani, slipping beneath the cool surface of the water. "You may drink of my water, but I am tired. I must rest."

Something dark and cold was coming to Havenwood Falls, and for the first time in centuries, Noelani was afraid.

Under normal circumstances, Stella might have been surprised to find a tall, willowy man with pale skin, long black hair, and even longer black fingernails holding a sign bearing her name at pickup in Denver International Airport, but goth subculture was in, and she never liked to judge someone else's fashion choices. Besides, in spite of the thick eyeliner around his deep-set eyes and the sharp, glinting points of various piercings in his face, he had a kind smile and a serenity about him that put Stella instantly at ease. She'd always thought the whole goth thing made people look angry and unapproachable, but the air around this guy was magnetic with an undeniably positive energy.

She hurried eagerly toward him.

"I'm Stella Malley," she introduced herself with a handshake, after triple-checking that the name written on the sign really was her own, which it indeed was. She was surprised to find she was out of breath, partly out of excitement and partly, she assumed, because of the thinner air this high above sea level. "And this is my fiancé,

Peter." She gestured in Peter's direction and gave a nervous sort of laugh that made her face flush. "I'm sorry, I hope we didn't keep you waiting. I didn't realize someone would be picking us up. I just assumed the shuttle ran on a schedule."

"It's not a problem at all, Stella," the man replied. His voice was serene and faintly dismissive, but the way he said her name was familiar—not overly familiar in a creepy sort of way, but in a way that almost felt like they knew each other from somewhere else, though Stella certainly thought she would have remembered meeting someone as unique-looking as this guy. She'd never met someone who wore more jewelry than she did before—at least, not a man who did. The pendant around his neck was particularly interesting, though—an hourglass that had sprouted angel's wings.

In quick, precise movements, he folded the sign and then tucked it away deep within the folds of his long black trench coat. His eyes made a quick dart to Peter and then returned to her as his lips curved into a small smile that gave Stella the impression it was meant just for her—and didn't include Peter. "We've been looking forward to your visit."

The flush on Stella's face warmed a little bit more, and she was glad that her skin tone was dark enough to hide the occasional blush. It made her feel both embarrassed and excited to be recognized, even if it was for a shuttle reservation she didn't remember making.

"I'm sorry," she said, "but have we met somewhere before?"

Stella ignored the sting of Peter's eyes in her peripheral vision.

"No," the man answered, "but it is a pleasure to meet you now, Stella. We're so glad you accepted the invitation."

"We?" Peter's voice, a little tighter than normal, cut in beside her.

The driver's smile flattened into a soft line as his eyes shifted away from Stella's. "Havenwood Falls, of course. It's nice of you to come along, Peter. Perhaps you will find something you are looking for in our little town, too."

Stella could sense Peter stiffen beside her, and the temperature in the space around him decreased by a few degrees. When Peter slipped into a foul mood, it was like he could suck all the air out of a place. She wrapped herself around his arm, sliding her hand into his to squeeze his fingers. "Kinda neat, huh, Pete? It's like the red-carpet treatment, just for us."

"If you say so." Peter's tone didn't hide his skepticism.

Minutes later, they were on board the shuttle, headed for the mysteriously hidden town of Havenwood Falls.

The driver, who'd said his name was Cicada, like the sweet-singing insect, didn't say much as they drove up into the mountains. His quiet wasn't unpleasant, though. Normally Stella enjoyed chatting up strangers, especially strangers who were as interesting-looking as Cicada, with his dark edges and multiple piercings. She wanted to know what the pendant around his neck meant—time with wings, she mused—but she was sleepy from the early morning flight. Soon the shuttle's smooth vibrations lulled her into an easy sleep as it chugged upward into the heart of the Rockies.

A few hours later, Stella awoke as the shuttle bumped its way past a stone welcome sign with beautiful black metal lettering that announced their arrival in Havenwood Falls. Her ears popped as the shuttle continued to climb for a few more minutes, curving a bend and cresting a ridge, before a gasp escaped her lips, stirring Peter back to consciousness in the process. He grunted sleepily and burrowed his head in her shoulder, but Stella moved to peer out the window.

From her new perspective, she could see all of Havenwood Falls spread out below as Cicada navigated down into the town. Excitement fluttered in Stella's chest as she took in the beautiful colors of fall that painted the town in vibrant hues of crimson and gold. She saw mountaintops and waterfalls, and the thought occurred to her that she might never again want to leave this place.

Perhaps that was what the pendant around Cicada's neck symbolized for her—it was time for her to fly.

CHAPTER 4

*I*t didn't take long for Peter to come to terms with the fact that Havenwood Falls was not going to be the quiet mountain respite that he'd hoped it would be. He'd feared this much the moment the strange shuttle driver had collected him and Stella, unannounced, from the Denver airport, and by the time he set foot in Havenwood Falls, he knew it to be true. He hadn't felt great about that Cicada character, either.

What was that weird symbol he wore around his neck, anyway? It gave Peter the impression that time was running out, which was not a pleasant thought. Between that and the weird makeup and black-on-black attire, the guy had the look of a grim reaper come to call.

Not comforting.

As the pair made their way through the town square, a strange thought struck Peter: if he let this town, it might drown him. It wasn't a happy thought, and not the first time such uninvited dread had invaded his mind. He'd managed to escape it for a while, but he seemed to be having a hell of a time avoiding it now.

The difference was that, this time, he wasn't going to listen.

For all its beautiful fall foliage and stony canyon walls—lovely, insulating geographic features that should have made him impervious to the uneasy sensation he felt around water, since there was so little of that here—Peter felt just as exposed in this hidden mountain ski town as he had on the wide expanse of sand and sea at his and Stella's home on the edge of the ocean. It wasn't the demanding, confrontational sort of sensation that had hounded him and made him lock himself away inside the ramshackle beach house that Stella insisted on renting. This was more of a surreal sort of feeling, one that shouldn't have made sense but was too real to ignore.

Peter indeed felt oddly suffocated, the kind of feeling one might get if they suddenly found themselves buried underground and were trying to claw their way up. Here he was, tucked inside the heart of a box canyon set deep in the Colorado Rockies and surrounded by mountains and dense forest—not a speck of open water in sight—and still Peter couldn't shake the feeling that he was being watched. Not by anyone in particular, but by everyone and no one. It was like dozens of little imps hid, hissing at him from their hiding spaces of rock and leaf and forest, their voices trickling to him in the sounds of the waterfalls that whispered in the distance.

No matter where he went—no matter how deep in the forest or how high in the mountains—the sinister voice of the water always found him. Even—and perhaps most especially—here, in Havenwood Falls. It was almost as if by going farther away from the voice, he'd come to its very source.

It seemed to like it better when Peter hid from it, too. It was too easy to taunt him when the thundering of waves could pound relentlessly against his thoughts like the hammering of drums, banging their way into his head night and day and day and night. Here they could whisper instead, teasing him from the rush of the waterfalls that gave Havenwood Falls its name in hushed, hidden voices that echoed sinisterly in the back of his mind and wound snakelike through the streams of town. It made Peter question whether the voice he heard in his head was theirs or his own.

Peter, the watery voices echoed, rushing back and forth like the sound of stirring liquid as they tumbled over themselves. *Peter, come to us.*

Then, more strongly, *Bring her to us.*

Peter shook his head, but the more the voices called, the harder it was for him not to listen. The sense of being watched closed in around him, pulling him under. He hadn't felt this way in over a year. Not since the accident—since Laura.

Come to us, Peter.

Peter shook his head, this time not to quell the water's voice, but to free himself from the memory of that day on the lake—the dreamy, maybe real memories he had never told another living soul.

Peter, the water called again, and this time it was Laura's voice that reached his ears.

Peter, help me, Laura cried, her voice shrill above the roar of the water. He saw her face again, pale and white beneath the blue. He put his hands over his ears, trying to block out the sound. Her lips moved underwater. *Pete—*

"Pete? Are you okay?"

Stella's bell-like voice broke through the maelstrom, and Peter turned to see her, smiling up at him with an expression of total innocence. His heart fluttered. He loved Stella, loved her more than anything or anyone he ever had. And that was what made her so dangerous to him. If he wasn't careful, the water would take her, too. Just like it had taken Laura. He wouldn't survive Stella's voice in his head, though. It would eat him alive.

"Yes," he self-corrected, forcing his lips into a smile. He squeezed her hand reassuringly and then pulled it away to rub at the stubble on his jaw. "Sorry, babe," he continued. "Just a little jet-lagged, I think. What were you saying?"

Ever patient, Stella smiled again, and Peter's heart thumped a little harder, grounding him solidly back beside her. Suddenly his head was clearer, whisper-free, and the soundtrack of Stella ambient in his head. Maybe what he'd told her hadn't been untrue after all—they'd barely had any sleep and were a couple hours behind their usual time zone. It was mid-afternoon in Colorado, but close to dinnertime at home. Bedtime was creeping up, and they still had a long day ahead of them. Stella's first gig was tonight.

"I was saying this place is just so pretty, isn't it?" Stella repeated, oblivious and talking excitedly. "I never would have guessed I'd love being in the mountains so much, not when I've always fantasized about living at the beach. But it feels so inviting here, like it was the town that invited me here more than the saloon. What about you? Do you like it?"

"It's great," Peter fibbed. "As long as you're happy, I'm happy."

Peter hated to lie to Stella, but as usual, he didn't have it in him to disappoint her. Though the town had escaped mention on every map he'd consulted, since he and no one he'd asked had ever seemed to have heard of it, it did feel disturbingly familiar now that he'd arrived. Stella had taken one look at the town and fallen—as was her habit—instantly in love, seeing only the quaint, picturesque storefronts and scenic landscape. Peter, on the other hand, had seen only a stretch of small businesses that looked like any other mountain tourist trap. It was funny how the same thing could look totally different when observed through another set of eyes.

Stella laughed and slipped her hand into his, tugging Peter onward down the sidewalk. He shifted his duffel bag to the opposite shoulder and took the handle of her suitcase so that she was free to peek, unencumbered, in every shop window they passed. Cicada—which Peter sincerely hoped was an unfortunate nickname that would be less permanent than the ring through his septum—had delivered them to the heart of the town square with a vague gesture in the direction of Whisper Falls Inn. The inn was located at the intersection of Eleventh and Main and, as the woman who'd taken Stella's reservation by phone had told them, would be the best place to drop anchor for their stay in town. It was centrally located and charming, and the luxury suite in the third-floor turret, Cicada added knowledgably—though Peter spied no obvious signs of a wedding ring on the man's finger—was a great place to spend a honeymoon night. The Haven Saloon was on the south block of the town square, at the western end. Cicada promised the walk between the two ends would be well worth their time after they checked in. That's where they'd find all that the town had to offer in its collection of bookstores, trinket shops, and eateries. After giving some recommendations on where to grab dinner if they wanted something more substantial than bar food, Cicada had disappeared back into his shuttle almost as mysteriously as he'd appeared.

Now, her hands cupped around her eyes as she peered into something called Madame Tahini's Potions, Lotions, Palm Readings, and Other Extra-Sensory Services, Stella's excitement was enough to shimmer in the air around her.

"Isn't this town just the most darling place you've ever been?" she gushed as Peter retrieved his fiancée from the window, guiding her gently on the route toward the inn. "I don't think I've ever seen a place that felt more like fall—fall and magic. It's even more beautiful than Rochester. This is the perfect place to start our happily ever after."

"Sure is," Peter agreed halfheartedly. It was easier than being disagreeable. He didn't mean to sound so sour, and he should have been happier—he was with the woman of his dreams, she'd agreed to marry him, and he planned to make her his while they were here in this beautiful little town she was so captivated by. He would have to get over the rest. It was all in his head, anyway. What else could it have been?

After a few more minutes of walking, Whisper Falls Inn appeared. It was, as Cicada said it would be, the quintessential small-town resort—it even had the kitschy gingerbread trim to prove it. A three-story Victorian-style manor, the large home-turned-inn sat diagonally on the lot, its wraparound porch facing the southeast corner of Town Square. It had turrets and bay windows, and the expanse of well-manicured lawn that stretched between the main building of the inn and the cottages behind gave it a well-loved appearance: old but not run down, comfortable but not pretentious.

Peter heard Stella's intake of breath beside him as her eyes landed on the inn.

"Wow," she cooed, mostly to herself.

The door chimed as they stepped in, and a woman behind the counter turned away from a small television set placed behind the counter to greet them. Peter glimpsed what looked like a cheesy Hallmark Hall of Fame flick—Glenn Close and Christopher Walken, wearing dusty colonial garb, argued over how to ensure their family survived a drought and then kissed with all the carefully choreographed passion a PG-rated romance movie could muster. Peter rolled his eyes.

He could seriously go for a drought right about now. Or a drink. Whichever came first.

"Welcome to Whisper Falls Inn. I'm Irina Petran," the woman behind the counter introduced herself. She had dark hair and green-grey eyes, and was cradling a baby in her left arm while she gathered registration paperwork with her free hand. She set the papers on the counter in front of Peter, then leaned forward to show off the child to Stella, who responded with precisely the reaction Peter would have expected. So far, his future wife hadn't brought up children—in fact, Stella had said she didn't know when, or if, she'd be ready for any—but that didn't keep her from gushing every time she saw one. "And this is Michaela," Irina introduced her daughter. "You must be Stella Malley"—her gaze drifted to Peter, pausing as if to drink him in and decide she didn't like the taste, then brightened—"and Peter Heilen."

Peter thought her voice was noticeably harder when she said his name.

"That's right," Stella said, her cheeks reddening. "That's us."

Irina smiled warmly. "It's about time we got a new singer at the saloon, and like I told you on the phone, there's nowhere better to stay in town than at the inn. You look like a singer," she added, her eyes sweeping over Stella. "If you sound half as much like Mariah Carey as you look, you'll be a star."

"I just hope I don't disappoint anyone," Stella said, blushing harder. "My first performance is tonight."

"I have a feeling that you will be spectacular," Irina said matter-of-factly. Peter got the distinct impression the woman was ignoring him. He didn't love it. "How long do you plan to stay in Havenwood Falls, Stella?"

Before Stella—or Peter, who had clearly been dismissed from the conversation—could answer, a group of people barged into the inn behind them, large cardboard boxes brimming with decorations in tow.

"Where do you want the banners, Irina?" one of them asked. Another flipped the lip of one of the boxes and pulled out a large fall garland of brightly colored silk leaves wound with sparkling copper tinsel. The third carried a sign that boasted the name Mara Blackwood in glittery calligraphy and her candidacy into something called Miss Teen Havenwood Falls.

"Anywhere you want to put them—go wild," Irina answered, motioning them back out the door. "Sorry about that," she said as she returned to her guests, accepting the registration paperwork from Peter without touching his fingers. "The whole town is preparing for the annual Founders Day festival this upcoming weekend. It's a big to-do, so everybody starts setting up days in advance so there's plenty of time to get it all done. We don't get a lot of visitors this time of year, though. It's mostly locals, so you two will be in for a treat."

Stella was obviously intrigued, though Peter would have much rather plucked out his own eyelashes than attend a local town festival in a town where he already felt out of place—and weirdly unwelcome. "What kind of festival is it?"

"Oh, a fall festival," Irina explained. "Vendors and games, that sort of thing—if you have time before going to the saloon tonight, you should explore the town square a little, watch everyone setting up. We crown one of the local girls as Miss Teen Havenwood Falls. Not sure who it'll be this year, but my bet is on Mara Blackwood." She peered down lovingly at the babe in her arms. "Not too long now and it might be you, huh, pretty girl?" she cooed to Michaela, who yawned as if festival pageants were the furthest thing from her mind.

"That sounds like a lot of fun, doesn't it, Pete?" Stella said, elbowing Peter in the ribs. Peter grunted. "You see, we're not just here so I can sing at the saloon—we're getting married, too—the sooner the better. So we'll have something to celebrate at the festival. Right, babe?"

Peter avoided Irina's eyes. Their color was, like everything else in town, just a little . . . off. Not totally normal. "Right."

"In that case," whispered Irina conspiratorially, leaning over the counter toward Stella while simultaneously sliding a room key in Peter's direction. He noticed it was for the turret honeymoon suite, even though they hadn't specified. "You might want to visit our wishing well, too."

"Wishing well?"

Irina nodded. "There's an old custom around town for young brides to visit the Lady of the Water that is said to inhabit an old wishing well out in the forest. If you visit her and wish for love, she will bless your marriage. Some people have even claimed that they've seen her, too. They call her Noelani—the mist of heaven."

"Oh, that sounds fun," exclaimed Stella, clapping her hands together. "Pete, we should go!"

Peter's response bordered on rude, though he tried to keep his voice even. "You want to go stomping off into the forest to ask a forest nymph to bless our marriage? Stella, babe, come on."

"Well, I think it would be nice," Stella insisted. "Not every newlywed couple can say they've been blessed by a Lady of the Water, you know. It would be so me, too—you know how much I love the water, Pete."

Peter knew. Somewhere in the back of his mind, he thought he heard that voice again, calling, calling. Dripping like a leaky faucet somewhere behind his eyes.

Irina smiled, but it didn't reach her eyes. She leaned closer in to Stella, so close that Peter couldn't clearly hear what she said next, but whatever it was made the sparkle in Stella's eyes dull just a little. Peter thought it must have been about him—why else would it be kept a secret?

Peter, help me, Peter, the phantom Laura voice cried again.

Irina was upright again, far away as if she hadn't just been whispering in Stella's ear. "Yes, you should visit her," the woman said in farewell as she turned back to her Hallmark movie, shivering as she pulled a blanket from the back of her chair over her shoulders so that it covered most of her and nearly all of the baby, "maybe sooner rather than later, too. There's an unnatural chill on the air. I think it might a cold autumn this year."

CHAPTER 5

*H*avenwood Falls was everything Stella had hoped it would be.

More, actually.

She'd known the town would be special when she first received the invite to sing at the Haven Saloon, and had kept her mind occupied before the trip by imagining what the town might look like. It had been a challenge, considering Stella had spent most of her life in upstate New York and had never even heard of a box canyon until she'd looked it up in the encyclopedia on Peter's bookshelf. But what she'd seen when she arrived had been so beyond her expectations that it felt like a dream, because places this beautiful surely didn't exist in the real world. While New York certainly knew its way around an autumn kaleidoscope, even the colors of the red oaks, maples, and river birches of her home state didn't compare to the phantasmagoric colors of this place. It was as if every season and color had added its essence to the town at once, with its vibrant fall hues set against the backdrop of silver mountaintops and distant waterfalls from which fell water bluer than the sky.

The mysterious little town hidden within the mountains felt like a secret; its off-the-map and out-of-the-way seclusion made

Havenwood Falls seem almost magical—a place of endless possibilities if only you knew where to look. Not to mention everyone she'd met so far had been so incredibly welcoming, as if they thought she belonged there.

Havenwood Falls, Stella was coming to believe, was a place where dreams might come true—where *her* dreams might come true —and she was more anxious than ever to find her happily ever after. A few hours in, she was beginning to get the feeling she might never leave Havenwood Falls.

Peter was—predictably—less than enthused. Stella could tell her sweet-but-grumpy fiancé was hesitant to let himself fall in love with the town like she had, but then he was always more reserved than her. The poor guy never seemed truly at home anywhere; sometimes Stella thought he looked out of place even in his own skin. He'd come around, though, she thought. He always did. Stella was the dreamer—the one with her head lost in the sky. Peter was her tether. Together they could see the stars without losing their footing. That reminded her of what Irina—the lady at the inn—had whispered in Stella's ear when they'd checked in: "Keep your eyes open," she'd said, "and your heart free. Beware of those who would hold you down."

After they'd checked in at Whisper Falls Inn, they unpacked enough to feel settled, showered, and—after a good bit of begging and more than a few pleading kisses—Stella had convinced Peter to take up Irina's suggestion and visit the town square. She wanted to take a peek at the Founders Day Festival preparations before introducing herself at the saloon and getting ready for her set. She hadn't been able to convince him to visit the wishing well. They had plenty of time, though—in fact, they had forever.

And Irina had said that young brides went, not young couples. Maybe she'd go by herself tomorrow.

On the short walk from where the shuttle had dropped them off, Stella had peered in through the windows of most of the shops on Main Street, but there was one in particular that had caught her eye—Callie's Consignments. The moment her feet hit the pavement outside the inn, Stella beelined to the store, Peter in tow behind her. As soon as she stepped inside, Stella forgot all about the beautiful natural scenery that formed the backdrop to Havenwood Falls and found herself instead immersed in what must have been a trip back in time to some other exotic corner of the world.

The store was a gypsy caravan gone retail. Like a mystical tent, the inside was much larger than the storefront had led her to believe, comprising two stories of mostly vintage clothing, furniture, and accessories. It was decorated top to bottom just as eclectically as would be the home of a wanderer who had collected treasures from all over the world over many lifetimes, with the peculiar furnishings and decorations as enticing and mesmerizing as the wares themselves. From the rugs that covered the floors to the interesting assortment of light fixtures and the lush, colorful fabrics covering the walls, no two items seemed to be the same. Everything was unique, as if the store had a mind of its own and it liked collecting things.

Stella was in heaven. If the town was magical, then this would definitely be the place she'd find her own pair of glass slippers or a dinglehopper or some other equally divine and powerful object. She'd brought her best dress, which she planned to use both as her debut dress at the saloon and as her wedding dress, but it seemed suddenly plain compared to all the curiously lovely pieces in Callie's.

Suddenly, she saw it, as if it had heard her thoughts and jumped out to surprise her.

Clinging to a mannequin at the edge of an aisle was the loveliest dress Stella thought she'd ever seen—and being a nightclub singer, she'd seen and worn a lot of sparkly dresses, from cheap prom dresses she'd picked up at thrift shops to cocktail dresses she'd snagged off clearance racks. This one looked like someone had spun the Milky Way into fabric and stitched it into an ombré-print dress with an angled bodice, banded empire waist, and full skirt. It was deep indigo with a layer of glittering pale pink, pinned with sequins that twinkled when they caught the light. This wasn't just a dress for a gig—and it wasn't even white—but it was something Stella could see herself getting married in.

It was prettier than anything she'd ever glued on her dream board, too.

"See something you like?" A rich, sensual voice vibrated in Stella's ear, making her start and then giggle nervously, embarrassed by her own jumpiness.

The woman the voice belonged to was as exotically beautiful as everything else in the store, olive-skinned with waist-length dark brown hair and curious hazel eyes. She was draped in silks and other textured fabrics that billowed around her slender frame as she moved, and she wore so many bracelets and necklaces that she jingled when she walked, as if she moved to her own music. A small tattoo peeked around the edge of her neck. Stella couldn't tell what it was, but she was sure it was just as interesting as everything else about the woman.

"I didn't mean to startle you," she said, edging closer. "I'm Lily Montgomery, owner and fashion consultant. Welcome to Callie's."

"Lily, like a calla lily?" Stella asked. Then, she got it. "Oh, calla Lily's—I get it!"

"Yes." Lily smiled, and the room seemed to warm with her. "My grandmother was the original owner of this story. She was Calla Montgomery, and it would seem the moniker stuck through the generations. But lilies symbolize luck and love, and so I would say there are worse things to be named for."

Nodding, Stella agreed. "My name is Stella."

"For the actress or the play?" Lily winked.

"Neither." Stella laughed. "For Stella Obasanjo, the political activist from Nigeria. My mom's people are from Nigeria, and she named me for Stella, because of her humanitarian work. I don't think I quite live up to it, though, or any of those other Stellas. I'm not a star like the Stellas that were actresses or the playwrights or even politicians. I think I was born to sing—just to sing. That's why I'm here, actually. I'm singing at the Haven Saloon."

Lily ran her tongue consideringly along her top lip. "There are different types of stars; they just all light the sky a little differently. Namesakes give you something—or someone—to be inspired by, but they don't determine the type of inspiration you can be. Besides, songs have their own kind of magic, don't they? They're just as important as the rest. They can lift you up, bring you down, inspire you . . . People need music. Giving it to them must be your gift— your own starlight—right?" She began to unbutton the dress, draping the fabric over her arm as it slid off the mannequin. She held it up, twisting the material so the dress sparkled in the store's ambient lighting, and then held it approvingly against Stella. "Either way, you need a statement piece, and I think this dress may have been destined for you."

Stella beamed as she regarded her reflection in one of the long dressing room mirrors that lined a nearby wall. "You think so?"

"Absolutely," Lily replied. "It's one of a kind. I look at this dress and I can see the stars—almost like a song itself. I think it suits you perfectly."

Stella and Peter left Callie's Consignments with the dress safely wrapped in a sleek clothing box, along with a pair of silver stilettos. Stella hadn't meant to buy the shoes, but when she'd put them on her feet, she'd felt like she was walking on starlight, and so it had been as impossible to leave the store without them as it had to pass up the dress. Peter had said she looked lovely in it, but worry lines still framed his eyes when he'd pulled his credit card out to cover the cost. Stella hoped she made enough tips to put his mind at ease.

The shopping excursion had taken longer than expected, and so it was nearly time for Stella to take the stage when they finally arrived at the Haven Saloon. She wished they'd had longer to explore the town, though, and her stomach was rumbling with hunger. Just as Irina had promised, Main Street was abuzz with vendors setting up their wares for the Founders Day Festival. Callie's had added a fall flourish to their windows, and, despite the *For Sale* sign in its window, a coffee shop called Coffee Haven had added festive signage to their doors, similar to the garland banners that Irina had been hanging at Whisper Falls Inn. If the activities that went along with the decorations were any indication, the festival was going to be the best place to be in town very soon.

A woman with short brown hair was arranging a station that offered temporary tattoos and tarot card readings on a table outside of the Haven Saloon. She was pale and pretty, wearing layers of flowing fabrics and a large crystal pendant around her neck. She instantly reminded Stella of Lily. Like Irina, she was nursing a baby in the crook of her arm.

Stella stopped suddenly at the table. Peter grunted as he collided into her back.

"What are you doing, babe?" he asked, curling his fingers gently around her forearm as he attempted to maneuver behind her to open the saloon door. "We don't have time to stop here. You're going to be late."

"Hang on," Stella shushed him, stepping nearer to the table while her eyes moved from the array of tattoo inks to the deck of tarot cards and the baby cooing in the woman's arms. "It seems like everyone in Havenwood Falls has a baby right now," she said by way of greeting to the woman at the table.

The woman's laugh sounded like windchimes. She stroked the child's cheek proudly. "What can I say? Life in Havenwood Falls goes with the seasons. Things bloom here in spring just like in the rest of the world. This is Addie."

"Oh, she's beautiful," Stella cooed. "Isn't she, Pete?"

Peter barely looked, but managed a small smile that looked passably pleasant. "Sure does," he agreed. He tugged gently on Stella's arm. "You're going to be late for your first night, Stel."

The woman with the baby shifted her gaze to Peter, and she didn't smile until she looked back to Stella. "Late? You must be Stella Malley, then? Welcome to Havenwood Falls. We're all very much looking forward to hearing you sing. I'm Lyra Beaumont. It's nice to meet you."

Stella felt her cheeks turn pink the moment Lyra recognized her name. Just like she hadn't expected the town to be so beautiful, neither had she expected such a warm welcome. So far, all the women she'd met had been as kind as family, which made Stella miss her mother even more than usual.

"Thank you so much," she said. "I'm so excited to be here."

Peter tapped his foot impatiently behind her.

"And right in time for the Founders Day Festival, too." Lyra swept her hand in front of her, ignoring Peter's obvious irritation. "How about a free temporary tattoo as a welcome gift?" she asked. "For both of you. Free of charge, of course. And it won't take long," she promised, looking over Stella's shoulder at Peter. "I promise."

"Oh my gosh, that would be amazing!" Stella exclaimed, thrusting out the inside of her wrist without hesitation. She already knew what she wanted. "Could I have a treble clef?"

"You got it," Lyra said. Handling the baby as naturally as if Addie were another appendage, Lyra spun a bottle of bright purple henna ink into the handle of her tattoo gun and began to trace the shape of the musical note freehand on Stella's skin.

It was a little warm, but didn't hurt. When it was done, Stella showed the mark to Peter, who rubbed nervously at his skin.

"Your turn, Pete," she said.

"Oh, I don't think so. Not for me."

"Come on, Pete," Stella begged. "It's only temporary—and it doesn't hurt a bit."

"That's right," Lyra agreed. "It's only temporary," she added.

Peter took another step backward, motioning toward the saloon. "Stella, your set begins in less than an hour. We really don't have time for this. Maybe we can come back tomorrow."

"Peter, please," Stella begged again, drawing out the *r* sound in his name. She batted her eyelashes and stuck out her bottom lip in her most pleading pout. When she noticed him start to soften around the edges, she gave a little squeal of delight, then reached out and wrapped her arms around him, shoving him forward toward the table. Oh, how she loved her handsome stick in the mud of a fiancé!

Grumbling, Peter stretched out his arm in acquiescence.

"Small," he instructed Lyra, and when she raised her eyebrow meaningfully at him, he added a "please" so as to not be rude.

Lyra changed the ink in her tattoo gun, swapping out the purple for a darker color that looked like a muddy brown.

"Any requests?" she asked, her tone expectant but curious.

"Dealer's choice."

In just a few minutes, Lyra was finished.

Peter lifted his forearm and glanced at his wrist, a quizzical expression turning his features. "A horseshoe?" he asked. "And a moon? Isn't that for good luck?"

"Yes and no," Lyra said, putting away her supplies. She turned back to working on her table as if the matter were settled. "The horseshoe is indeed a symbol for luck, but it has other uses as well."

"Like what?" asked Stella.

"Protection," Lyra answered without elaborating. Addie cooed agreeably.

Peter was still studying the mark on his arm like he didn't like it. "Protection?"

"Yes, protection." Lyra laughed, the windchimes stirring again. "It comes from a practice in ancient England, back before the years numbered into four digits even. There was a blacksmith named Dunstan, who was later canonized. Anyway, legend says that he nailed a horseshoe to a horse, only it wasn't any old horse—it was the devil in disguise. The horseshoe caused the devil great pain, and he made a deal with Dunstan: if Dunstan removed the shoe, the devil would never enter a house that displayed a horseshoe. And so it became a symbol of protection from evil . . . which I guess you could say is one of the greatest tokens of luck."

Stella clutched Peter's arm and gazed at the symbol with newfound appreciation. "And the moon?"

"Ah, the moon," Lyra continued, raising a finger toward the sky. "Well, that's where Artemis comes in."

"Artemis the Greek goddess?" asked Peter.

"Artemis the moon goddess," Lyra corrected. "She was the patron and protector of young girls, and was worshipped as a goddess of childbirth. That was Addie's addition, wasn't it, baby girl?"

Lyra jostled her arm, and the baby giggled as if in agreement.

Stella expected Peter to grump about being given a tattoo that had anything to do with having babies, but to her surprise, he laughed. "Well, the good luck I appreciate, and how could I turn down the protection from evil? But the moon and childbirth? I think your daughter might have misjudged her audience."

"Oh, maybe." Lyra shrugged. "But not all tattoos we get are for ourselves, are they? Even the temporary ones. The question is, Peter —are you the one giving the shoe, or the one who should wear it? And what would the moon see if she should look down?"

CHAPTER 6

*P*eter had been distant and temperamental all afternoon, but luckily Stella had been too distracted with exploring the town's tacky stores and gimmicky festival setup to take notice. He couldn't believe he'd let her talk him into getting a tattoo, though, even if it was a temporary one. Peter hated tattoos, almost as much as he disliked the water, and he wasn't too sure how he felt about being branded with a horseshoe or a moon. But Stella was like that—once she got an idea in her head, it was nearly impossible to get her off of it. It was easier just to give in.

Like always.

Anything for Stella. Stella, his bride to be. Stella, the girl of his dreams. Stella—

Peter.

Peter swiveled at the sound of his own name whispered darkly over his shoulder, but the only thing behind him was a door, and it was closed.

The moment they'd entered the saloon, Stella had glimpsed the sign for the ladies' room with the uncanny knack that most women had for finding that particular safe space in places like pubs and bars, where men had the habit of lurking about like sharks eager to feed. She'd been bubbling with excitement and, muttering

46

something about dreams coming true, had taken off to change into her new dress—the one that cost nearly as much as her engagement ring—before introducing herself, leaving Peter to stand around alone, holding on to her handbag lamely like a fish pulled out of water and plopped in the bottom of a boat.

Why hadn't he just stayed at the inn, Peter wondered to himself. No, he had to be here for Stella's first night—he wanted to be here. This was her big shot, right? The first time she'd been invited to sing somewhere, rather than throwing herself on the mercy of dinky pubs and off-the-beaten-path taverns that paid her in peanuts and leering glances. Though, if he was honest with himself, while Peter wanted to be around for Stella, he'd rather be anywhere other than here—a sentiment which applied both to the Haven Saloon and the entire geography of Havenwood Falls. The scant hour they'd spent in their honeymoon suite at Whisper Falls Inn had been a merciful reprieve from the foreboding sense of doom that had followed him from Florida and descended in earnest once they'd arrived in town. The whispering, watery voices he'd been hearing had attacked again with renewed vigor when he and Stella had set about the town square, and they seemed to grow louder and more insistent every time they edged nearer to the falls or the forests.

It might have been a figment of Peter's imagination, though he'd never had a terribly good one and didn't know why he'd start now, but he'd imagined that the voices had grown loudest just before that Lyra woman had etched a horseshoe on his wrist. He could barely remember anything that had happened in the clothing shop before pulling out his wallet, but his head had gone mercifully clear the moment he'd been tattooed. Branded, like some common animal. Or at least it had been clear, lasting a full five minutes until he'd heard his name on the breath of nothing. And Stella had been wrong: the tattoo was weirdly painful; it seemed to hurt worse now than it did during the application.

Peter.

Peter shook his head and resisted the urge to look behind him again.

The Haven Saloon was just like everywhere else in town that he and Stella had seen thus far: a blend of weird and bizarre that tiptoed the balance between quaint and touristy. The place wasn't nearly as seedy as most of the joints Stella sang in, but it wasn't exactly the Ritz either. They way Stella reacted, though, one would have thought it was the Taj Mahal. The two large windows that flanked the entry had already been plastered over with flyers for local happenings—most of which were concerned with the upcoming Founders Day Festival that Peter was already sick of hearing about.

What little light was left of the afternoon sun filtered in through slanted windows, which looked like they hadn't been cleaned in a while. Peter suspected this might have been intentional to add to the saloon's mystique, rather than just sloppy housekeeping. The bar itself was clean enough to reflect the glow from the few pendulum lamps and wall sconces that illuminated the otherwise dark space. The décor was something between rustic and industrial, devoid of the exotic flair that had given the vintage clothing shop its personality. Compared to Callie's, the Haven Saloon seemed downright glum—dim and smoky and just a little sad.

And it reeked of pot.

The cherry on top, though, was the owner, some dude named Brent that Peter just couldn't—insert sarcasm—wait to meet. Peter was beginning to sense a theme developing around the inhabitants of Havenwood Falls: all the women wore flowy clothes and were preoccupied with babies and oversized jewelry; all the men gave themselves terrible nicknames.

Peter scoffed, feeling momentarily superior for reasons he didn't want to think too deeply about. He eyed the horseshoe on his wrist and wondered why that woman had really chosen that symbol.

Because you are different, Peter. The water's voice breathed almost invitingly this time against Peter's ear, like it offered better company than the pitiful handful of people in the saloon. *Come to us.*

With another shake of his head, Peter moved farther into the bar, away from the dirty windows where someone—something—

outside might see him. Then, without deciding to do so, he tugged the sleeve of his shirt down over his wrist, cupping his hand to keep the fabric pinned safely beneath his fingers. He never should have let Stella talk him into that silly tattoo. He didn't like the burning sensation where it was on his skin, either. Maybe he was having an allergic reaction to cheap ink or something.

"Hey there," called the man behind the bar, Peter's sudden movement having caught his attention. "Can I getcha a beer?"

Resigning himself to what he could only assume would be an absolute bore of an evening, Peter perched on a barstool, as far away from the other single occupant of the bar as he could without coming off as rude, and eyed the labels of the bottles behind the man's long mane of dirty blond, shoulder-length hair. There was an insane amount of vodka, particularly the flavored kinds—colorful bottles containing every flavor from apple to zucchini lined the bottom row of the liquor shelves.

Peter grunted in disapproval. He still hadn't figured out why flavored vodka had become a thing, much less why the fad had taken off with such a vengeance. What was so wrong with plain vodka? The rest of the shelves were lined with wine bottles bearing the label of someplace called Stone Falls Winery, which Peter had never heard of but thought was probably local—and probably made by a woman in a flowing dress and her man, Wicked Willy, or something.

Peter cracked his neck, hoping he could break the bad mood along with the pressure in his joints. Between the early flight, lack of sleep, and general moodiness, he was even getting on his own nerves.

"What'll it be, man?" the guy behind the bar planted his palms on the bar top, and a bold wave of cannabis infiltrated Peter's nostrils. He exhaled away the stench, but had no doubts about its origin. The guy certainly had the look of a stoner, outfitted in layers of flannel and featuring glassy, slightly pink-tinted eyes.

"Moosehead if you've got it, Miller Lite if you don't," Peter decided, trying not to sound glib. The bartender pulled a bottle of

Heineken from under the bar—of course they wouldn't have anything non-domestic—popped the cap, and set the bottle and a frosted glass in front of Peter. "Thanks."

"New in town?" asked the bartender. Still feeling unavoidably irritable, the question struck Peter as annoyingly invasive rather than friendly bar banter.

"Just visiting," mumbled Peter. He took a swig of Miller Lite, then another, tapping the bar top to signal he'd need a second. At least the beer was cold and tasted normal. Peter felt a little guilty for being so standoffish. No wonder the women Stella had met so far in town seemed perfectly content with acting like Peter didn't exist—like if they ignored him well enough, he'd just fade away completely. He didn't exactly want to become friendly with anyone, but it was sort of nice to be acknowledged. "My fiancée is singing here," he said, inviting further conversation. "She's just getting ready now. Know where we can find the owner?"

"Right here," the bartender grinned dopily, pointing two thumbs backward at himself. "I'm Brent. The locals call me Bent Brent. Welcome to Havenwood Falls, man."

Peter swallowed his reaction in a bigger-than-necessary gulp of beer. *Of course you are*, he thought.

Just then the sound of heels tapped their way up behind Peter. Half a second later Stella's warm hand was smooth and reassuring on his arm. Her touch soothed him in a way the beer never would, and he felt the tension coiled in his body ease just a little under her hand as her voice swept over his shoulder like a lullaby.

"Hi, Brent. I'm Stella," she introduced herself, having apparently overheard the exchange. "Thanks so much for inviting me. I hope I'm not late."

Brent's glassy eyes sharpened instantly, and the single other patron sitting at the bar turned his head and—at least in Peter's approximation—made a point of taking in his view of Stella with all the subtlety of a hungry wolf who'd just stumbled across a tasty morsel alone in the woods. Anger flared in Peter. He could barely tolerate the women they'd met, whispering secrets in Stella's ears; he definitely didn't appreciate the men eyeing his soon-to-be wife like some kind of delicacy.

Stella's finger squeezed into his shoulder, and he resisted the urge to jerk away from her. He knew what she'd say if he shared his thoughts with her—and no, he wasn't imagining things.

Above his head, the evening was moving on without him.

"That's right!" Brent palmed his face and then grinned, extending a hand across the bar and breaking Peter's view of the man at the other end. "Almost forgot you were coming in tonight, silly me." Brent laughed like he found his own forgetfulness hilarious. It wasn't. "But glad you're here. Welcome."

He gave Stella's hand a quick shake and then he swept his arm over the open expanse of empty tables and sagging booths. "It's a little slow yet, but night'll be picking up soon. Lots of the crowd that hangs in here doesn't get out much until the sun goes down— but then we got ourselves a real party." He jerked his head in the direction of the other man. "Ain't that right, Rusty?"

The hungry wolf at the other end of the bar, whose name apparently was Rusty, raised his beer in agreement. He smiled, and it might have been a trick of the light, but Peter could swear the guy gave him a mocking wink. His vision went red.

"You're welcome to get your bearings up on stage," Brent went on, pointing toward the small stage at the opposite end of the room. "Mic's all set up and whatever music you want, I'm sure we can queue up for you."

"I brought my own," Stella's voice returned from Peter's side, where the indigo fabric of her dress sparkled in his peripheral vision. He felt pressure on his arm as Stella dug around in her handbag, which Peter had forgotten was still hitched on his shoulder. He flopped it onto the stool next to him right as she lifted out a handful of cassette tapes and a few slim CD cases.

"Then the stage is yours to command, my lady. Let me know how I may be of service." Brent offered a playful salute. "Go on and settle in. We can sort the paperwork later."

All three men at the bar stared after Stella as she made her way to the other end of the room, a vision in her sparkling starlight dress. Even Peter held his breath as he watched his bride-to-be tinker with the stereo system and fuss around with the derelict-looking sound equipment. He hated to admit it, but that gypsy woman at the dress store had been right—the dress did look like it was destined for Stella. It fit her perfectly, the fabric hugging and flaring in all the right places, and the blues and pinks of the material made her lovely caramel skin all the more creamy, the dark curls of her hair all the richer and more vibrant. The lipstick she wore tonight was the same pink as the top layer of her dress, and Peter yearned to kiss it away from her lips.

Peter sipped his beer as he gazed at Stella, forgetting entirely his overwhelming desire to be surly as he drank in the view of the most beautiful woman he'd ever seen—until he noticed he wasn't the only one staring at Stella with stars in his eyes.

Bent Brent had returned to doing things that bar owners did—scrubbing down bar tops and polishing glass and not cleaning windows—but the man at the other end of the bar was looking at Stella like he might want to take her home. His dark eyes tracked her every move, and with each flicker Peter felt his temper kindle, then ignite, and then begin to flicker hotly within him.

Peter sized up the man—Rusty, wasn't that his name? Peter's theory about the men of Havenwood Falls and their nicknames fluttered into his thoughts. He noticed Rusty's hair was the same reddish-brown color as oxidized iron itself, and wondered briefly if his moniker was just another unfortunate nickname. Either way, this guy was no walking goth stereotype like Cicada or pothead like Bent Brent. Peter considered Rusty. He looked like he was probably close to Peter's age and his own six feet in height, but where Peter had earned most of his muscles from the gym, this guy looked like the kind who'd earned them outdoors, especially if his jeans, hiking boots, and flannel shirt that looked like they might have been borrowed from Brent's closet were any indication.

If it came down to a fight—and if the burning sensation at the back of Peter's throat was any indication, it might—Peter wasn't sure he could win.

"Something I can do for you?"

For a second Peter thought it was the water talking, until he realized that Rusty's lips had moved. Once he realized this, he became aware that, just as Brent had said, the bar had become suddenly populated. Not just populated, but crowded. He even caught a few familiar faces. Lyra—who had neither her tattoo gun nor her baby—and the woman from the dress shop were both looking intently in his direction, staring at him, Peter thought, the same way he'd been boring holes in the side of Rusty's head. Lyra turned to whisper in Lily's ear. She nodded in agreement with whatever the other woman said. Both moved closer to the stage—toward his Stella. He got the impression they were trying to cut her off from him, to keep him away.

Peter.

Peter recovered quickly, and returned his attention to the more pressing problem. Women could gossip all they wanted, but if this guy thought he was going to get between Peter and his fiancée, he was dead wrong. Raising his voice so that he'd be heard over the din of excitement that had begun to fill the air as the bar's new patrons chatted and clamored amongst themselves, Peter did his best to mark his territory. "I was just about to ask you the same thing. Noticed the way your eyes were feasting on my fiancée."

"By the moon!" Rusty exclaimed. "I'm not looking at your girl, friend."

Peter did not like being called names any more than he liked bad nicknames. "I'm not your friend, friend."

The temperature in the room fell to subzero as Peter made as if to stand up, but that was the moment when Stella began to sing. The effect was as if the room had spun into orbit, and her voice was gravity. It rang out, loud and confident, over the crowd, capturing everyone's attention instantly.

"By the moon!" Rusty of the hungry eyes exclaimed again, and Peter had to agree.

His Stella was a star. And she would always, always be his.

CHAPTER 7

*N*oelani sat in the underground cavern that was her home, counting the flower petals she had collected from the offerings brought by those who visited her well. She arranged them in various manners as she considered the ways the coldness had altered them. Some had curled edges; others still wore frost spots in their centers. Such a sudden change, she knew, meant that something was coming. This was the way of natural things; the cycles of seasons both figurative and literal.

Change was positive or negative, but very rarely neutral. The cold made Noelani nervous. It meant, at worst, that the chill of death was coming. An ending, cold and final. At best, it implied stasis—a form of debilitating stillness or an otherwise abrupt and lasting pause.

Neither was a terribly promising omen, and Noelani was not accustomed to such dark thoughts. She only wished she knew what it was for certain, but since she almost never left her well and rarely had any company whom she might ask, she knew little about what went on in the world around her. For the most part, that was just fine. But since the unseasonable cold had found its way to her well, she could not escape the worry that the change that was upon Havenwood Falls was intended for her. There was a new imbalance in the box canyon, and nature would correct it even if magic could not.

Noelani thought of this and grew even colder as she counted the petals, and as she did, she heard something that sounded like music, high in the sky above her well.

It was not the singing of birds or the strumming of an instrument, but something even more beautiful—a tune with a quality she had not heard in ages. She tipped her head to the side and listened.

It was not music at all, but song.

A woman's voice, as elusive and melodious as the chime of brass, carried bell-like on the wind from the epicenter of Havenwood Falls, somewhere amid the town square, from which Noelani caught the faintest whispers of voices and music, and sometimes magic. The sound filtered down through the cold, dark waters of Noelani's well. It filled her ears, delicately, and with it came a rush of warmth that stole away the chill in her heart.

Despite her lamentations, Noelani liked what she heard. She floated to the top of her well, pulling herself up on its stone brim where she sat, listening intently.

The musical quality of the woman's voice reminded her of the celesta, a French instrument with a name that shared meaning with Noelani's own. Her namesake was the mist of heaven. The celesta's name was derived from the French word celeste, meaning heaven itself. It was as fitting a name for the instrument as for the voice that breathed warmly against Noelani's heart, melting the frost in her hair and smoothing away the goose bumps on her flesh.

"Celesta . . . celesta." Noelani enjoyed the feel of the word as it played on her lips in time with the woman's song, and then another slid from her tongue.

"Stella."

CHAPTER 8

*B*y some strange twist of fate, Peter grew more tense and agitated at the exact same rate at which Stella became happier and more enchanted with Havenwood Falls. At some point, possibly very soon, she worried they'd both go so far around that they'd swing back in the other direction—and either crash into each other or die of whiplash in the process.

The couple had been in town barely three days, and the polar opposite ends at which they normally orbited had never before felt as far apart as they did now. What had been a quirky, opposites-attract type of relationship—the kind Paula Abdul had famously sung about—now felt empty, stretching endlessly between the two of them in a black, ugly void that grew wider every hour. Stella had felt the tension starting to grow the moment they'd stepped off the plane in Denver, but she could almost put a timestamp on exactly when the distance had started: the moment Cicada had greeted them at the shuttle.

Peter had begun slipping away from her during the drive into the mountains, and by the time she'd walked out of the ladies' room at the saloon and touched his shoulder, the man she loved had felt like a stranger beneath her hand.

She remembered how he'd felt. Hard and foreign. Almost

untouchable, like the mannequin that had worn what was to be her wedding dress before she'd bought it at Callie's.

The old wisdom Stella's mother had shared with her before she and Peter had left Rochester the summer before had come back to haunt her. "You barely know him," her mom had warned. "No good can come from running away with a man you barely know." With those words, worry wormed its way into Stella's bones. She and Peter had only been together a little while, in the scheme of things. She deeply loved him, but did she truly know him?

It wasn't something she'd ever considered, but now that she had, Stella didn't think she did. She knew what Peter liked for breakfast (poached eggs on an English muffin) and how he took his coffee (black, two sugars). She knew what papers he liked to read (the *Times*) and how he looked fresh out of the shower (perfect). But she knew little about his past, nothing about his family—she wasn't even sure why he'd pulled off the road and wandered into the Skylark the night they'd first met, much less what he'd been driving toward—or away from. She'd asked once and he'd said, "Nothing," and they'd left it at that.

Suddenly that nothing felt a lot like something, and Stella had been trying to shake that feeling ever since she'd first realized she felt it. She'd drowned herself in songs day and night to keep her heart from growing heavy from the burden of worry, like she always did when she felt out of her element. So far she'd gone through four sets of batteries and her voice was growing hoarse.

And it wasn't working. She was sinking quickly, and Peter was not only falling away from her, but he seemed to be pulling away. Like he was trying to get as far away from her as possible.

"This town creeps me out," Peter had said when they'd returned home after her first gig. "I feel like everybody here is watching me— like they know something about me that I don't or something. And it's bad."

"You're imagining things," Stella had protested. "Everyone is so nice and welcoming."

"To you," spat Peter. "But then you're the star, aren't you? I'm just the dumb horse you rode in on." Here he'd brandished the temporary tattoo Lyra had given him at her like it were an exhibit in a courtroom.

Peter hadn't joined her last night for her set at the Haven Saloon, where Stella had worked her way through the songs that were her staples—several of Mariah's, Vanessa Williams's "Save the Best for Last," and even a number by Celine Dion called "Water from the Moon," which Stella had never sung before, but it called to her when she saw it in the saloon's song index.

The lyrics asked if the singer must do the unthinkable—find water on the moon—to make their lover's heart come back to them. When she'd sung that, it felt like the words were her own—the ones she'd been searching for and trying to say to Peter but hadn't known to put together.

She'd never even heard the song before, but the words had hurt when she'd sung them, and any relief she'd found from the burden of her newfound unease dissolved. It wasn't that she thought Peter didn't love her—no, it wasn't that at all. It was something else. Between the aching feeling of disconnect and the niggling doubts spurred by her mother's words, Stella couldn't quite put her finger on what was wrong, but even not knowing exactly what bothered her didn't stop the worry from chewing at her insides. She felt constantly queasy, on the edge of losing her cookies.

When Peter worried, he got angry. Apparently, Stella got nauseous.

None of this not knowing had ever bothered her before. Stella had always been of the mind that she and Peter were creating a future together, not reliving their separate pasts. But as Peter's mood continued to sour, the words Irina Petran had whispered in her ear when they'd checked in two days ago—keep your eyes open, and your heart free—no longer felt inspirational, but more like a warning. Cicada's necklace, the hourglass with wings, likewise suddenly didn't feel like dreams taking flight, but time flying away. And even though Stella was happier than she might have ever been, a chill had begun to seep in through the pores of her skin—turning everything, from her upcoming wedding to the songs she picked for her set, cold.

Now, not only did Peter feel like someone she didn't know, but she was beginning to feel afraid, as if not only was he a stranger, but a dangerous one. Cold feet were one thing, but this wasn't at all what love, and dreams coming true, was supposed to feel like. That much, at least, she did know.

Stella thought again of the wishing well in the forest, the one she'd been told belonged to Noelani, the Lady of the Water who could bless their love. Every time she'd tried to bring it up to Peter over the past two days, he'd only gotten angrier and more frustrated. It began with statements that she should focus on practicing new songs for her ongoing engagement at the Haven Saloon, a practical, if useless, argument—Stella easily knew at least a hundred songs by heart. Eventually, Peter began to make strange comments about getting lost in the woods or falling into a stream, but these were odd, paranoid types of things that were utterly contrary to the avid outdoorsman she knew Peter to be. In the time they'd been together, he'd never met a mountain he couldn't climb or a trail he couldn't trek.

But when he'd raised his voice and yelled at her—something he'd never done before—she'd given up asking altogether. He'd just not been feeling well, he said. Headaches and the like, he'd insisted while clawing at his own head. She'd dropped the subject faster than she expected Mariah Carey to dump her manager-turned-husband Tommy Mottola.

As Stella watched the sun rise through her window where she lay beside Peter in their hotel bed, she shivered. The autumn morning waking up outside didn't look crisp and beautiful like it had when they'd first arrived in Havenwood Falls. It looked cold and rainy and gross. But even if the weather wasn't perfect, Stella told herself, today was the Founders Day Festival, which meant that tomorrow was the day they'd planned to get married. With this thought firmly in her mind, Stella hesitated only briefly before she pounced on Peter, peppering his sleeping profile with kisses.

She'd also reached a decision: she'd go to the well on her own to ask the Lady of the Water to bless their love. Stella wasn't particularly superstitious, but then she wasn't the type of girl to ignore such a nice idea, either. And who knew? Havenwood Falls was magical enough; maybe there was something real to the legend. Maybe all Peter needed was just a little bit more love to pull out of his darkness.

"Wake up, sleepyhead," Stella said softly, working her way from Peter's jaw to his lips. "It's festival day. Wedding eve."

Moaning in his sleep, Peter wrapped his arms around Stella and rolled her under him, attempting to cuddle her into submission. "Let's just stay here," he mumbled, voice thick with sleep. "Go back to sleep."

Stella wriggled away from him, only to climb atop him, straddling his body as she kissed her way down his throat to his chest. He moaned again, but even though his eyes stayed closed, other parts of his body were definitely waking up beneath her. That kind of reaction Stella recognized, and when one of Peter's eyes peeled open to gaze up at her, she felt a little silly for thinking he could ever be a stranger. His eyes were the color of fresh grass in the morning, nostalgic and refreshing at the same time.

"Are you sure you want to go back to bed?" she teased, drawing out the words while she tickled her fingers along his ribs. She pulled at the waistband of his pajama bottoms, pulling away and then flicking the elastic band against the solidness of his abdomen.

Peter's moan turned into a throaty growl. His left eye opened just a little and his hands slid upward to cradle her hips. "Well now I think I just want to stay in bed. With you."

"Oh, you do, do you?" Stella laughed. She slid her body lower onto his so that she could press her weight against him.

"I do." His voice was breathy. It was the first time since they'd gotten to Havenwood Falls that he sounded like her Peter again.

"Too bad, mister. It's the Founders Day festival today," Stella reminded him. "And you promised we could go, so let's go. Up and at 'em."

Peter's mood instantly shifted.

"I don't want to go, Stella. I don't want to go out there." His voice was hard and flat. He nudged her off of him and slid from the bed, disappearing silently into the small washroom. Stella waited as he took care of his morning business and then came back into the room, moving right past her to the small desk on the other side of the suite, where he lowered himself into a chair without so much as looking in her direction.

Any enthusiasm Stella had dared allow herself to feel evaporated instantly. She pushed herself upright, shivering again. This time she tried to rub the cold—and the irritation—out of her skin with her hands, but her fingers were like ice on her already cool skin, and the whole exercise just made her colder. Like Irina had predicted, the temperatures outside had indeed grown cooler—unseasonably cool, even this high in the mountains—and, like the widening gulf between them, seemed to have a direct correlation to Peter's bad mood. Stella bundled herself in an extra layer of blankets as she glared across the room at Peter, who sat, shirtless and totally comfortable, and as distant from her as the moon.

"Why?" she asked, when it was clear that Peter wasn't going to bother to explain himself—or say anything at all. He had a strange expression on his face, and when he did finally look at her, he blinked a few times, as if he hadn't recognized her.

"Why do you even want to go so badly?" he snapped. "It's not like this is our home. That woman downstairs said it was mostly locals at the festival anyway. If you haven't noticed, we don't live here. We don't belong."

Stella huffed. "We may not be locals, but we're here, aren't we? We've met people. We've made friends—or at least I have. You seem to want to fight everyone who looks at me for some reason."

Peter's left eye twitched. He glowered at her but didn't say anything. A shadow moved across his face.

"I don't want just to go to the festival, Pete," Stella sighed eventually. "I want to go with you. I want us to have a great day together. We're getting married tomorrow, and right now I sort of feel like that's not what you want anymore."

"I never said that. Of course I do." Peter's voice cracked like his tongue was under the tremendous strain of things unsaid.

Stella twisted her engagement ring on her finger. She'd done it so much that the flesh was starting to get raw and crack. "You didn't have to. If you've changed your mind, you can tell me."

"I already told you: I don't feel well."

"I just don't get it," Stella confessed, not ready to let the issue go until she zeroed in on the source of the problem. Now that she'd gotten him talking, maybe she could get him to actually tell her something. "You were fine before we left Pensacola. It was your idea to come here—to come with me. But ever since we got here, you don't want anything to do with this place. God, Pete, it's like you don't even want to have anything to do with me. You say it's not that, but what else am I supposed to think?"

On the other side of the room, Peter had the audacity to roll his eyes. Stella considered grabbing her robe and storming out, but two heartbeats later, Peter beat her to the tantrum. He flew out of his chair as if attacking the air between them, his fingers splayed as his hand reached toward her.

"The whole reason we're here is for you, Stella. The whole reason I'm still here is because of you. I can't get away from it. And I hate what it's doing to me—do you have any idea what you are doing to me, Laura?"

Stella flew backward in the bed as if he'd hit her. Who the hell was Laura, and what exactly was Peter so desperate to get away from?

An hour later, Stella stood at the edge of the forest, thinking dark thoughts and willing her heart not to break in her chest. She clutched the glass music box in her hands and the gold of their wedding bands glinted in the sunlight.

She and Peter had never had a fight before. Not a real one. They'd bickered a lot, and occasionally one or the other had gotten snappy, but Stella couldn't remember a moment when she'd ever felt so miserable with Peter. An argument she could chalk up to wedding jitters. Maybe even a small fight could be written off to the stress of being in a new town, away from home, and pent up together in a hotel room. Perhaps Peter did feel sick. It could have been something he ate, or the thin mountain air this high above sea level.

But none of that made him calling her by another woman's name in a fit of rage anything near acceptable. If he'd been anyone else, Stella would have ripped the jewel off her left ring finger and flung it straight out of the window, or flushed it down the toilet. In any case, it would have been off her hand and she would have been out of there, headed right back up to Rochester, where she could tell her momma that she'd been right. Nothing good had come of running away with a stranger—just a lot of hurt and heartache and disaster.

It might even make a good song, Stella considered. Heartbreak was always a chart-topper.

She had been so angry that she could barely speak when she asked Irina directions to the wishing well before she left Whisper Falls Inn on foot. So angry that she'd barely heard Irina's response, or whatever had come after it. She seethed the entire taxi ride to the forest, arguing with herself through every possible recourse to that thing in her hotel room who had stolen her fiancé from her. Just who in the hell did he think he was? It wasn't like he had a secret identity that had sprung loose the moment they got to Havenwood Falls, although it sure as hell felt like it.

Eventually, Stella's anger had given way to despair, and then, by the time the town square had faded into the distance behind her, to guilt. Was this her fault, Stella wondered. Had she asked too much from him? After all, it was she who had received the invitation to come to Havenwood Falls. Maybe he hadn't been meant to come.

Maybe this was her journey, and Peter never should have

followed her here. She loved him—that wasn't in question, even now. But maybe she should have taken the gig and enjoyed the fall alone—kind of a bachelorette party before the wedding where she could have one last thing for herself.

But she hadn't done that, obviously. Peter had come, and whatever was troubling him—whatever it was that was "doing something" to him was her fault. Or at least, it wasn't not her fault.

By the time she'd been dropped off at the edge of the forest with simple instructions on which trail to follow to find the wishing well, Stella had almost abandoned the whole trip through the forest. She'd not-so-briefly considered that she should get right back in the car, drive right back to Whisper Falls Inn, collect her things and her love, go home, and put this whole thing behind them. She stood and stared at the brilliant colors of the forest unfolding before her, and the only thing she wanted more than the blessing of the Lady of the Water was just to go home. It wasn't a blessing that she needed anyway; it was to go back in time.

Half a dozen songs queued up in Stella's head.

Stella laughed to herself. There truly was a song for every occasion. She'd just assigned a third meaning to Cicada's pendant, too. If she saw him again, she'd have to ask which one was right. She turned to begin the walk back to the town square and stopped, frozen in her tracks.

There was a wolf—a large, shaggy animal with fur the color of rust—standing right there, in broad daylight, staring at her. It didn't growl or appear particularly menacing, just watched her, its tail wagging ever so slightly. Even odder, it looked familiar, and Stella was positively certain she'd never met a wolf before.

Something that sounded like *oh my god* tumbled out from between her lips. Stella swallowed and took one step backward. Two. The wolf stepped forward. Three.

"Nice wolf," she tried, patting the air in front of her in supplication, hoping that the animal would turn and walk away, go back to doing whatever wolf things wolves typically did during daylight hours. The hardness of the asphalt driveway under her feet gave way to the soft crunch of dew-crisped grass. Peter's eyes flashed into her memory.

Stella swallowed again, her mind not letting her forget that the wolf stood, unmoving, between her and civilization.

"Nice wolf," she tried again. "Now go on; go ahead and run away. Leave me alone."

The wolf cocked its head to the side as if curious, but it didn't turn away. Instead, it took another step forward.

Stella hummed as she tried to quickly sort out her next move.

The wolf growled. It lunged.

Stella turned and fled into the forest.

CHAPTER 9

*H*e couldn't believe he'd called her Laura.

Couldn't. Freaking. Believe it.

Of all the things he could have said to Stella—all the things he arguably should have said—anything would have been preferable to that. Why that? He was losing it.

Peter, the water's voice whispered, grating against the inside of his mind like nails on a chalkboard. He could no longer differentiate the ghostly whisper of the woman he'd accidentally—no, not accidentally—yes, accidentally—drowned in the lake in Shenandoah National Park any more than he could the falling of water from the faucet in the bath or the rain that fell endlessly from the sky. He'd loved her too, Laura, hadn't he? Not as much as Peter loved Stella, but he had loved her.

He hadn't wanted to hurt Laura. He still couldn't believe—wouldn't believe—that he had. It hadn't been him. Not really. It was the water. Yes, the water was to blame. It called to him, told him to do terrible things. Forced him. It whispered to him whenever it was near, and no matter how much he tried to ignore the sound of its call, it forced its way into him. It changed him, turned him into something else—something that he never asked to be. He'd been running from it since.

A gross shiver of pleasure raced through Peter as he remembered the reflection of Laura's face shimmering below the water as it drank her up. The look in her eyes. The memory swelled in him, excited him as it stirred deep in his body and dark in his heart. Desire flooded through his veins. Peter gasped, horrified and delighted at his own reaction. He hated what he had done, and craved it with a longing he did not have the words to describe.

Come to me, the water called. *Bring her to me.*

"Shut up," he commanded, pressing both hands against the side of his head so hard, the pressure made his jaw ache. The horseshoe tattoo on the inside of his wrist flared painfully. He wanted to scratch it off his arm, scratch at it the way Laura's hands had at his face when he'd held her just far enough below the water that she couldn't reach him, one hand atop her head, fingers curled tightly in her pretty red hair. It had been so quick, lasting just for a moment —scratch, scratch, scratch—and then her body had gone soft and her hands had slackened. Then she had fallen away, drifting downward, slipping into the water's throat as it swallowed her.

Peter forced the memory away. That was long ago now. Far away. He'd been running from it—from the water—ever since. He'd been trying to get as far away from the water, from himself, as possible. But now it had found him, here, of all places—deep in the mountains of Colorado. It had tracked him down as slowly and surely as a river found its way back to the sea, and now it wanted her, too.

Stella.

Peter hadn't meant to lose his temper with Stella. He wasn't even angry with her. He was the very opposite of angry: terrified. He couldn't make the voices stop, that constant rush of moving water that beat like waves and whispered like puddles and pinged like raindrops inside his head. It raged and swelled like a storm over the ocean, and Peter was powerless to do anything other than be flung about like wreckage in the maelstrom, tossed to and fro on the waves as they rocked him.

The water wanted Stella, and it wanted him to give her to it.

But he wouldn't. No. She was his! Peter wouldn't let the water take Stella! He would keep her safe . . .

He would keep her safe. He just needed to keep her away from the water, that was all. He needed to keep her somewhere dry, yes, and more than anything, he needed to get out of Havenwood Falls. It had been a mistake to come here. This wasn't an ordinary town; he'd known that the moment they arrived. There was something else here. Something that knew what he was—

A monster who fed his loves to the water.

All his life, Peter had heard stories about such creatures. Myths about sinister beasts that could adopt the shape of animals and would drag women down into the depths, drowning them. They had been given many names in many lands, these beings. Some were seen as mischievous, others as playful and sometimes cruel, but only one was seen as truly evil.

The horseshoe on Peter's wrist burned. He heard the sound of hooves pounding like drums inside the roar of the ocean.

Bring her to us, Peter . . . Peter . . .

Nykur.

He regretted letting Stella walk out of the hotel room more than any other terrible thing he'd ever done the moment the door shut behind her. She'd stormed out—rightfully so—and to add salt to the wound, Peter hadn't even bothered to chase after her.

Not at first, anyway.

For a while he'd just sat right back down in his chair and stared at the space on the bed where Stella had been. She'd been right there, with tears in her eyes as she'd practically begged him to come to her, just as earnestly and beautifully as the water had been begging him to come to it.

And oh, how he'd wanted to! He'd wanted to take her up in his arms, to cover her in kisses and assure her that everything was fine. Everything would be okay. They just needed to leave this place, that was all.

But he hadn't, had he? No. He'd looked at her, and the hate he'd felt had been every bit as strong as the love. It was her fault this was happening, Peter knew that, even if he didn't want to believe it. It was her voice that had lured him off the road, she that pulled him into her gravity and would not let go. She'd tricked him into loving her, and now he was addicted to that love. He saw how brightly she shined, how everyone around him looked at her, as if she were every star in the sky and he was nothing more than the backdrop of darkness that gave her space to shine. If it hadn't been for Stella Malley, Peter would never have let himself fall in love again, and if he'd just avoided that, then he wouldn't have to suffer.

Well, if Stella insisted on making him suffer, then he would have to make her suffer too. He'd wash the shine from her. Dull her light so that it wouldn't blind him.

Peter.

The tattoo on his wrist flared and stung, the mark coming to life as if Lyra's tattoo gun was hot upon his skin, stabbing the horseshoe into his flesh. The pain was so strong, it pushed the voice of the water out of his head.

In the sudden silence, the heat receding from his wrist, Peter flung his arm out over the desk, sending the table lamp and phone book clattering noisily to the floor. This was madness! Peter wasn't sure what was going on in his head. Stella had suggested it was wedding jitters. Maybe it was the lack of oxygen. Maybe it was both, or something else. Peter didn't know. He just knew he needed to get to Stella—to make her his before he lost her forever.

The woman at the front desk of the inn hesitated before telling him that Stella had gone to that blasted wishing well in the forest—the one where the fairytale lady in the water supposedly granted wishes to young brides.

"Perhaps you should wait for her here," Irina suggested. Her eyes landed purposefully on the mark on his wrist, like she'd known its meaning all along. "Or maybe you should leave Havenwood Falls altogether. Stella is happy here. We will keep her safe."

"She's not in danger," Peter snarled, furious at the implication that he was the danger, though deep down he knew it was true. "And she is mine to protect."

He left the woman with her baby, stumbling through the town square that was decked out for the festival. It seemed like everyone in Havenwood Falls was there, packed into the small area so that he had to weave his way around the bodies of the town's residents. He caught glimpses of familiar faces—the woman from the dress shop, the bar owner, the woman who'd given him the tattoo.

Peter recognized their faces, but couldn't remember their names. His head was full of noise that he could no longer hear clearly, and his senses were overwhelmed to the point of overload. The scents that infiltrated his nose didn't make any sense. Everywhere he turned, pushing through the throng of Havenwood townies enjoying their festival, he smelled animal—things furred, feathered, fanged. He scented things, too, that had no smell. Things he shouldn't have even been able to discern as there at all found their way to him, and Peter got the feeling that all of these were working together, trying to trap him amongst them.

Trying to keep him from getting to Stella.

At one point Cicada appeared before him, but Peter shoved the man aside and kept going.

Pete. It was her voice he heard now, calling him to her the same as it had done the night he'd pulled off the road in New York.

He wasn't sure where he was going, but his feet carried him steadily toward the water. The thought of traipsing out in the woods —of being anywhere near any sort of water, even if it was a well— did not sit well with Peter, but if that was where Stella had gone, then that was where he would go.

It was freezing, but Peter barely felt the cold as it wrapped around him. The deeper into the forest he walked, the more frigid the air became, blowing against his back as if it were following him. When the cold had become so unbearable that his muscles clenched and his bones began to ache, Peter saw her, standing with her back to him.

He could see Stella's profile as she whispered into the well, and then he saw it.

The water.

It lapped over the edge of the well, running in cool lines down the stone sides just the same as the tear that slid down Stella's profile.

Peter saw the water, and it saw him, and everything he had been running from caught up with him.

Nykur.

The tattoo on his wrist scorched as if a red-hot brand had been laid against his skin, but even the excruciating pain of the mark was not enough to overcome that which spread suddenly throughout his body. His arms and legs stretched into long, muscled limbs beneath him, and his blond hair turned as white as the cold around him as it fell in shimmering waves like sea foam down his skin. The agony was excruciating as his body reformed, his bones cracking and reshaping even as his mind screamed out for it to stop, and by the time Peter's hands rested upon the ground, they were no longer the hands of a man, but hooves of a horse.

CHAPTER 10

$\mathcal{T}$he second the wolf had lunged at her, Stella fled into the woods, all thought of abandoning her trip to the well forgotten.

Since then she hadn't stopped running, the rubber soles of her sneakers finding purchase on the earth as her feet carried her deeper and deeper into the densely packed foliage of Havenwood Falls. The forest passed in a brilliant flash of colors around her—blushing sweetgums, blazing chokecherrys, golden aspen with white trunks—but Stella saw none of it. For a while it had felt like she would never stop running, even though she had long since ceased to hear any signs that the animal still chased her. There was no growling, no padding of paws on the ground, nothing that should have compelled her to keep running, but nevertheless she could sense danger pressing in behind her back, and so she ran.

Stella ran, and she hoped whatever it was didn't catch up to her.

In her fright, she hadn't paid attention to where she was going. The smooth, well-trodden path of the trail had long since given way to uneven, unblazed terrain that was peppered with jagged edges of sharp rock and roots that stretched upward like hungry fingers from under the earth. Branches grabbed at Stella, scratching her face and arms. Twigs tore at her clothes. She fell once, but ignored the sting in her knee and kept going, wincing through the pain. Even when stitches stabbed her sides and her breath came in great, ragged plumes of frozen air, she kept running. She ran so far and for so long that the silver walls of the mountains that surrounded Havenwood Falls began to loom up before her, deepening the canopy of trees into shadow, and she knew eventually she'd run out of space to flee.

Eventually the walls of trees broke apart into the slim shapes of spindly, uneven aspens through which she could see sunlight, and at last even these gave way to the tall, brushy grass of a wildflower meadow. Stella kept running, more slowly now so that her own momentum carried her. At last, when it felt like she couldn't take one more step, the vision of the well rose up before her, and the forest bloomed into color and scent again. It was cool here, not cold as it had been in the forest, but the crisp, inviting kind of coolness that one might feel as they slipped between fresh sheets on the first night of spring.

Stella's feet slowed beneath her. She moved more cautiously now, more out of anticipation than fear, setting one foot tentatively in front of the other. Her hands grazed the tops of the wildflowers as she walked amongst them, her fingers pulling petals until she had to cup her hand so they didn't spill from her fingertips. The forest was quiet around her, but not still—she could hear the tinkling sound of water, like the babbling of a brook, before her. And then, very faintly, she thought she heard a woman's voice, singing somewhere on the wind. It was the most beautiful sound she'd ever heard, befitting for a Lady of the Water who dealt in love and blessings.

The well, as it stood before her now, was just as Stella had imagined a real wishing well might be. A peaked cedar canopy hovered above a yawning mouth of gray stone, and with the bright midday sun shining down, the unassuming round shape appeared carved out of sunlight. It glittered like gold, and Stella shielded her eyes with one hand as she leaned against the well, angling her body so that her feet anchored her to the ground but she could still bend forward far enough to see the water all the way to its bottom.

"Noelani," she whispered into the water, when her pulse had slowed and she breathed evenly again. "I am here to see the Lady of the Water. I am here to ask for your blessing."

Stella peered into the water of the wishing well and let the petals tumble one by one from her hand into its depths in offering. Their sweet, heady scents seeped into the water, and the fragrance rose up to meet her. For a while, though, Stella saw nothing, and her heart sank. Had she really expected the legend to be true—that some lovely creature truly inhabited these waters and granted blessings to those who wished for them?

Yes, she had, because it was the only thing left she knew to do. She had to believe, because she now knew that the man she so desperately loved was falling away from her, and this was the only thing left she could think to do to save him.

"Please," Stella pleaded, her voice cracking as the first tear slipped from her lashes. "Please, Noelani, if you're there, please hear me. I really need your help."

When it seemed that it had all been for nothing and Stella finally loosened her grasp on the stone brim of the well's edge, something stirred far below. A shape, red and white like strawberries and cream, floated to the top and hovered just below the surface. For a moment, a cloud of crimson billowed like ink dropped into a pail of water, and then it cleared, bringing into view a woman's face.

Stella gasped at the sight. The woman in the water was beautiful, like something out of a dream that was too perfect to be real but still undeniably there.

"I am the Lady of the Water," her lips said, and though Stella couldn't hear the woman's voice, she could feel it washing over her, warm and comforting like bathwater. Stella felt something pass between the two of them as she stared into the woman's emerald eyes—a sort of peaceful knowing and shared secret that instantly connected them in an unbreakable way. "What is your wish?" she asked.

Stella lifted the music box that was still clutched in her hands. She had kept her fingers curled tightly around it as she ran, and it was almost painful to loosen their hold.

"I am to be married," she explained, "but my fiancé, Peter . . . something is wrong."

Noelani's face turned sideways in question.

"Wrong?" she echoed.

"It's like, he's the sky, right? Only where the sun used to be, there's a dark cloud that's passed over it. Peter is still there, trapped behind it—I know he is—but the cloud has taken away all that was warm and bright and made it cold and dark and distant." Stella fumbled for words to explain the darkness that had come over the man she loved. She'd barely even acknowledged this, and the words to describe it hadn't even formed completely in her head yet, much less her mouth. "Something is bothering him, but I don't have any idea what it is. I can feel it, and whatever it is is dark. Dangerous," she admitted. The sensation of being chased fell over her again, and she shivered.

Noelani said nothing.

Stella licked her lips, feeling silly but strangely resolved. She held out the music box to Noelani but kept it just above the surface of the water so as not to damage the mechanism that made the box chime. "The lady at the inn where we're staying told me that you give blessings—that you bless people's love. I was hoping that you could bless ours—mine and Peter's—and we might be happy again."

"That is true," Noelani's lips moved again. "But my magic blesses love that already exists. It makes it brighter, stronger . . . but I'm afraid it does not change love."

"Change love?"

"If darkness has crept into your love's heart, even when it is clear that you love him so strongly and so brightly already, then I fear nothing I can give you will help," she explained. "I cannot grant love, and I cannot make love that is received different than what is given."

"But he loves me," Stella insisted. "I know he loves me—just as

76

much as I love him. I just need him to remember—to come back to me."

Noelani nodded, and she rose a little higher so that her features were more sharply defined and Stella could see clearly the outline of her lips as they broke just above the water. Her voice was a whisper. "Not all love is pure," Noelani warned. "Some love is dark. Some love is drowning. You must run away from it, Stella. Run away—do not let him trap you in a love that is, above all else, loveless. Keep your heart free."

Keep your heart free.

Stella opened her mouth to say something, but as she did, she saw Noelani's face twist into fear. The Lady of the Water pushed back below the surface, descending swiftly into the safety of her well. Stella heard the crunch of grass behind her, but before she could turn to see what brought the shadow that had fallen over her shoulder, she had time for one more thought—Peter—and then the world swallowed her and all was icy, cold, and dark.

CHAPTER 11

*N*oelani's heart ached at hearing the hurt in Stella's words. This was the imbalance that had come to Havenwood Falls—the change that had turned her waters cold.

Stella was pure love—bright, shining, and blue—but even her light was not enough to illuminate the darkness of the man she loved. It wasn't exactly magic, but love that powerful had a way of transcending into something that was very much like it. Noelani didn't know how any darkness could be so bleak as to be impervious to such a blinding light as what Stella's love offered, but whatever it was, it was tainted and cruel, a darkness that could only come from a very black sort of soul.

Noelani knew instantly why the magic of Havenwood Falls had called to Stella. It had been trying to save her, to call her home where she might shine brightly without being smothered. And she had come, but the darkness had followed her, clinging to her in the nasty way that shadows always clung to the edges of dawn. Stella had come to Noelani's well to ask for her blessing, but for the first time she would not be able give it. It was a test for them both—for Noelani to understand the boundaries of love, and Stella to know when to love herself more than to give her heart away to someone—something—that did not deserve it.

Noelani had known this, and so "Keep your heart free" was what she told Stella when the woman asked for her blessing.

Stella dropped her head in resignation, and then she parted her lips to say something as a shadow rose up behind her, eclipsing her as totally as a moon sliding across the sun. Whatever she might have said was lost. Her eyes went wide, and she was shoved so quickly and so suddenly into Noelani's well that her scream filled the water.

"Peter! Peter, stop!" Stella cried, her voice growing at first more panicked and then strangely sleepy. When her throat had filled too fully with water to form words, it was simply the sound of her grief that carried on the water, and the feeling of such pain and misery pierced Noelani's heart even more sharply than Stella's words had.

Stella's scream shattered the peace of Noelani's well, and Noelani screamed with her. She could taste Stella's grief, but could do nothing but watch in horror as a dark figure forced Stella's head beneath the water. It held her there, rigid and unrelenting, as she screamed and thrashed, her arms and hands tangling in her own hair as they fought to free themselves of the thing that held them trapped underwater.

Noelani screamed again, calling out for all those magical in Havenwood Falls to hear. To come. To save Stella's light from being extinguished, and to rid the forest of the darkness that had followed her here.

But no one came. It happened so quickly.

Stella stopped screaming. The silence was deafening, and then a sound . . . The music box had slipped from Stella's hand and opened, spilling the pair of wedding bands into the water. A haunting melody chimed from the box as it sank to the bottom of the well.

"Let her go," Noelani yelled, choking on Stella's grief where it polluted the water. Exhaustion overtook her as she reached for Stella. Noelani pushed all that she had—all the magic she could give—into the water's essence, not to bless Stella but to save her. To give her life, breath, anything that would allow her to escape from the monster at her back.

Mouth gaping, Stella's final words were a whisper in the water. "I loved him," she confessed, as the rich amber of her skin paled into milky white and the sparkle in her eyes burnt out. "Peter."

The moment Stella died, the water began, finally, to freeze. Her body went slack and then toppled completely into the water, pushed into its depths by the monster who'd drowned her. Fury wrapped itself around Noelani as she gathered up Stella in her arms and held her body against hers, clinging to the brilliant, beautiful star whose shine had been blown out so violently.

Stella was gone, and even though Noelani had known her but minutes, the weight of that loss destroyed her. But even worse was what she saw next, staring down at her in the depths where she clung to Stella's drowned body and waited for the cold to claim her. At first Noelani saw the shape of a great beast, white-hot with rage, and then it moved, shimmering in the way the vision of an oasis might glimmer in the desert. When she blinked again, it was not a beast that she saw staring into her well, but a man.

Noelani saw him, Peter Heilen, fair of skin and hair but black of heart, and she knew what he was. She could smell the scent of animal and knew exactly what sort of beast drowned women who loved them.

"Nykur," she growled up at him, glaring at his downturned face. "What have you done?"

Drips of water still fell like falling tears from his fingertips as Peter's eyes locked on her. "I didn't mean to. I didn't . . ." He fumbled for words, looking momentarily lost before the weight of satisfaction fell over him. "She made me," he insisted. He wiped at his face and then abruptly jerked his eyes upward. "I had to drown it out."

Noelani tried to look away, but it was too fast. He saw her, his eyes spearing hers where she stared upward at him, still clinging to the body of Stella Malley, and just as Stella's last words had been the name of the thing that drowned her, the face of Peter Heilen was the last thing that Noelani saw.

CHAPTER 12

*W*hen Peter came to on the now-frozen ground beside the well, he knew what he had done. Worse, he knew now he would do it again if given the opportunity—not because the voices made him, but because he had liked doing it. He had enjoyed the feel of holding Stella under, of feeling her love for him as it bled out of her into the water. Still, he was filled with self-loathing. He had loved Stella, loved her every bit as much as he had loved killing her.

It was in his nature, the evil inside him as much a part of himself as the part that loved Stella so fiercely. He had never meant to harm her, but it had been foolish to think that he would not. His love, no matter how well-intended, was twisted and cruel, and Peter resolved in that instant never to love again—and to never, ever again put himself near enough that he would hear the call of the water. He might not be able to resist its call, but never again would he let it claim someone he loved.

"Stella." He said her name one last time and then ran from the forest, the limbs of the trees scratching at his skin as he fled on bare feet back to the town. When he broke through the last barrier of trees, he was surprised to find a congregation of familiar faces awaiting him, as well as others he did not recognize.

They looked expectantly at the tree line, and it was impossible to miss the grief and disappointment that washed over them when they saw it was Peter who emerged from the forest, and not Stella.

Lyra Beaumont was the first to speak. "Where is Stella?" she asked.

The others—Rusty, Lily, and Irina, as well as an older, severe-looking woman—stared at him, their malcontent evident in their eyes. Peter didn't know what to say, so he said the only thing he could. "In the forest. At the well."

He didn't bother to clarify that she was now *in* the well, and—mercifully—no one challenged him. It's not like they would find her body anyway, not without dredging the well, and he doubted the . . . *thing* . . . that lived in it would allow such a thing.

Irina turned her head into Lily's shoulder, and Lyra's face went white. "I had hoped the magic I put into your tattoo would be enough to restrain your evil from coming loose before Stella could seek the wisdom of the Lady of the Water," she said. "And I hope now that her magic may be strong enough to heal what is broken between you.

"The magic in the tattoo?" asked Peter, remembering the way it had burned and stung on his arm, as if it had been a brand. "What are you, some kind of witch?"

Lyra glared at him. "Some kind of witch, yes."

"And we know what you are," added Rusty. "And what you are capable of doing."

"You have taken magic tonight. Magic that was not yours," Lily cut in, touching her fingertips to her forehead as if seeing by an inner eye. "It is the magic of the Lady of the Water. She has blessed you?"

Peter felt his eyes narrow. Again, he did his best to evade the question. "The woman in the water. I saw her."

"Yes, Noelani." Lily looked to Lyra.

"What does this mean?" Lyra asked. "We had expected her blessing to go to Stella, not Peter."

"It is difficult to know, but it cannot be a good thing."

Peter was quickly losing the thread of the conversation. The women talked amongst themselves, but Rusty's eyes remained locked on Peter. Peter had the impression that if he made a run for it, it would not go well for him.

"What happens now?" he asked eventually.

For a moment, the congregation of people barring his escape from the forest stared silently at him, and then the other woman, the one whose name Peter did not know, spoke sternly. "You were never meant to come to Havenwood Falls, Peter Heilen," she said. "The invitation was for one. Stella will stay with us. You will leave this place now, and you will never return. And the magic you have stolen, every bit as much as the love that you have blackened, will haunt you for the rest of your days. Eventually you will wither and dry out, and become as starved for love as the women whose hearts you've drowned with your own evil. Now go."

One by one, they cleared a path for Peter. Cicada waited at their backs, the shuttle door open behind him. Peter saw his bags had been brought from the inn and were waiting on one of the seats.

Unsure of any other action, Peter moved toward the shuttle. He set one foot atop the first step of the shuttle's stairs, and only then did he move his eyes up to face the man who would ferry him away from Havenwood Falls. So tall that he still rose above him even on the shuttle's step, Cicada didn't speak, and he didn't smile. Whatever warmth had animated the man when they'd first met was long gone. He seemed little more than a statue now, cold and indifferent, though he still wore the same strange pendant around his neck that had been there when he'd first delivered Peter and Stella to Havenwood Falls three days before.

The hourglass no longer stood on its base, but was turned on its side.

Peter had to clear his throat twice before he could speak. "What does it mean—that thing around your neck?"

Cicada's black eyes drifted upward to Peter. "It means time, at least for some, has stopped."

Peter gulped in fear. An unfamiliar and decidedly uncomfortable sensation shot like fire in his veins.

"I am a nykur," he admitted, speaking the word aloud for the first time. He jerked his hand in the direction of the people still watching from the edge of the forest. "One of those women is a witch. And there was a woman living below water. I don't know about the others, but they're definitely not human." With every word, the fear dug deeper into his bones, burning him in a way that the tattoo never could. He could barely force the next words off his tongue. "What are you?"

Cicada grinned then, the smile slicing apart his lips and curling far too high up on his gaunt face to be anything other than terrifying. "One day you will find out. One day I will come for you, ready to drive you to another place, the place where you truly belong. But today is not yet that day, Peter Heilen. Not yet."

EPILOGUE

$\mathcal{I}$n the wake of the events at the well, a dark curse was born.

A vicious cold spread fast and violently in the little corner of the forest that had belonged to Noelani, the naiad who once gave blessings of love and light from her waters. When it did not thaw and none of the spells cast could warm it, that area of the forest was erased from maps and guarded by the protection of the Court of the Sun and the Moon, the town's governing council, so that no innocent soul would wander into the woods and find themselves lost in the dark. Noelani's well was abandoned, and what was left of the Lady of the Water was no longer a thing of love and blessings, but a monster of darkness and decay.

She became the rusalka, and all—at least for a while—was lost. Noelani would wait in the darkness for a light bright enough to burn through the never-ending dark. One day the magic of her well would return, but until then she would wait, and dream, and wait. No one disturbed her, not even to recover the body of Stella Malley, because sometimes it must be from the very ashes of loss that something new can be reborn.

Peter's deceit was eventually discovered, and though he had already fled, the wards were sealed off behind him so completely that even if, on some long-away day, he remembered the magical little town in the heart of a box canyon high in the mountains of Colorado, he would never be able to return.

And so it was, and for many years, so it would remain. In the days to come, Peter's black heart would wither and dry within him, and Noelani would wait. Still, though the love of Stella Malley was gone, it would not be forgotten. She would shine on, a single star in the darkness, until one day, from the very unlikeliest of places, her light would break through the curse of the drowning bride.

We hope you enjoyed this story in the Legends of Havenwood Falls series featuring a variety of supernatural creatures. The series is a collaborative effort by multiple authors. Find out what happens with Noelani in *Of Salt and Stars* by Seven Jane.

Books in the historical Legends of Havenwood Falls series:

Lost in Time by Tish Thawer
Dawn of the Witch Hunters by Morgan Wylie
Redemption's End by Eric R. Asher
Trapped Within a Wish by Brynn Myers
Blood and Damnation by Belinda Boring
Fated Beginnings by E.J. Fechenda
Emeline by Katie M. John
Released From a Curse by Brynn Myers
A Pack of Lies by Kallie Ross
Kiss the Ashes by Desiree Lafawn
Hidden Truths by Colleen Nye
Wrath and Retribution by Belinda Boring
Changing Fate by Char Webster
Rise of the Witch Hunters by Morgan Wylie
The Drowning Bride by Seven Jane

Also try the main Havenwood Falls series; the YA line, Havenwood Falls High; the darker, sexier side of town, Havenwood Falls Sin & Silk; and the local supernatural college, Sun & Moon Academy.

Stay up to date at www.HavenwoodFalls.com

Subscribe to our reader group and receive free stories and more!

ABOUT THE AUTHOR

Seven Jane is a bestselling author of dark fantasy and speculative fiction. Her debut novel, *The Isle of Gold*, was published by Black Spot Books in October 2018. She is represented by Gandolfo Helin & Fountain Literary Management and supported by Smith Publicity.

On Facebook, Twitter, and Instagram @sevenjanewrites or at www.sevenjane.com.

ACKNOWLEDGMENTS

Many thanks are due to Kristie Cook, Regina Wamba, Liz Ferry, and the team at Ang'dora Productions, as well as to the many wonderful authors whose stories have contributed to the incredible world of Havenwood Falls—most particularly Kristie Cook, E.J. Fechenda, Susan Burdorf, and Randi Cooley Wilson, whose characters welcomed Stella into Havenwood Falls 1993. I am so grateful and proud to be a member of this fantastic community.

AN EXCERPT

- A Havenwood Falls New Adult Novella -

HAVENWOOD FALLS

OF SALT AND STARS

SEVEN JANE

Continue the story of Noelani and the Heilens in *Of Salt and Stars* by Seven Jane.

Two women, one love, and a curse lurking in deep, dark waters.

For as long as she can remember, Maris Heilen has been haunted by dreams of a beautiful woman beckoning to her from beneath the water. These dreams have been Maris's only constant. She's lived her life like a leaf caught in the rushing tide: no rules, no commitments, and no long-term lovers, either—just a string of broken hearts that have tried to anchor her unwilling heart to the earth. When her dreams take on a new sense of urgency following the mysterious death of her estranged father, Maris knows it's time to uproot and keep moving, her soul pulled to the west, toward the water—toward *her*.

Instead Maris finds herself drawn to a surreal little town high in the Colorado mountains, where she begins to believe her dream might be much closer to reality than she'd ever imagined. When she discovers her past is linked to a legend even more haunting than her dreams—and that the woman in them is not only real but in danger of being lost to an unfathomable darkness—Maris resolves to outshine the evil that has crept into a small corner of a forgotten forest in Havenwood Falls.

OF SALT AND STARS

BY SEVEN JANE

MANY YEARS AGO

At the edge of the lush green forests that surround Havenwood Falls, where the sweet-smelling junipers and majestic pines tickle the walls of the silver snowcapped mountains that border the town, in a place seldom traveled and even less often remembered, there once stood a well.

It was a well of the wishing sort, with a peaked cedar canopy that hovered above a yawning mouth of gray stone rendered soft by the breath of innumerable years. The well was one of those rare structures that during the day appeared carved of sunlight, its golden shine so blinding that the only way to look upon it was to shield one's eyes and sip it in quick glances lest it steal your vision completely. At night, however, the well was perhaps even more beautiful, when under the glow of a silver moon it seemed as soft and elusive as the stuff of dreams, formed into being by the twinkling of a thousand stars. Regardless of the time of day, the air always seemed more fragrant near the well—scented by day with a pomander of wildflowers and by night with the heady flora of thistle and night-blooming jasmine. So tangible, too, was the magic in this place that the air was always just a little cooler here—a wrap was necessary even during the hottest parts of the year—and it was so quiet that the whisper of the clear water that swelled nearly to the well's lips could even be heard above the rustling of the forest itself.

The animals that lived in the surrounding wood did not drink from the well, nor was its water harvested as drinking water for the town. Indeed, no bucket was ever hung from the awning from which to draw, for those few who knew of the well also knew that it was enchanted, and its waters imbued with a very special sort of magic. See, the well was not merely the fount of a spring. Far below the water's surface, in a hidden lake in a cavern below the earth, dwelled a creature as temporal and beautiful as the structure itself— a naiad by the name Noelani.

The naiad's well was a carefully guarded secret in Havenwood Falls, and only a few knew of its location, but those that were lucky enough to know the well's secret—most often women but occasionally men and children as well—would visit. There they would cut their hair and cast hushed wishes to Noelani, the Lady of the Water, and dip long wooden spoons into the well for a sip of her water's magic.

Most of the well's patrons—both human and supernatural alike —wished for love, for like other naiads, Noelani was a spirit of such things. Young girls were keen to look for their beloved's reflection hovering under the wildflower petals that floated on the well's surface. Older—but no less lovestruck—young brides garbed in their wedding dresses came to collect vials of Noelani's water, which brought them fertility. And when their bones began to ache, elderly women in their widow's habits sipped spoonsful of the well's water for vitality. If one was lucky, they might even catch a glimpse of the naiad herself, alight on the well's brim under the glow of the sun or the full moon, her long red hair swirling in the water beneath her as she sang songs more beautiful than those of the sirens at the banks of the waterfalls on the other side of Havenwood Falls. If this were the case, then the person would have been even more richly blessed, for it was said that whoever's eyes met Noelani's would be granted the gift of her magic, and some of her love would remain in their hearts forever, making all of their days blessed and sweet.

For many years, the naiad's well was a place of good fortune for all who visited. Noelani was happy, and her water was pure. But that was long ago, and such lovely places rarely endure for long— even those so consumed with love, for love is the most fickle of all beasts.

The opposite of love is not hate but jealousy, and it was this that caused the well to ferment and the magic of Noelani to become diseased. It was jealousy of the ugliest kind—that which bleeds from the eyes and can sour milk just by the look of it—that led to the death of a young bride by the name of Stella Malley, who, on the very eve of her wedding, had come to ask the naiad's blessing and instead found herself drowned by the man who'd promised to marry her.

The manner in which he killed her—some say he held her head below the water until her lungs filled all the way to her throat, others that he strangled her with the train of her veil and sank her body with stones—is less important than his reason for doing so. The root of his this man's darkness was jealousy, not of what he couldn't have—for Stella had promised to be his—but of what he couldn't *control*. With her long black hair, creamed honey skin, and black eyes that sparkled like stars, Stella was as lovely as the midnight sky. But even more charming than her face was her heart, which drew others to her in droves and caused her to outshine the man who would have been her husband, and—had such a thing been possible—her shadow.

The man—his name important only because it is on the list of those that have been banished from Havenwood Falls, and such things are sparingly done—was a Mister Peter Heilen. And when Heilen forced his betrothed's face into the naiad's well, Noelani watched, helpless from below as Stella thrashed, the poor girl's lungs filling with water she could not breathe. As precious moments passed, Noelani saw the light inside Stella's eyes grow dim and faint until it burnt out altogether, and when the richness of her skin had been replaced with the gray tinge of death, her face relaxed and her mouth fell open.

Only Noelani heard Stella's final scream, and the sound was so anguished that when it infused the water, it also filled the naiad's heart with rage. With Stella's scream in her stomach, the naiad shrieked, her beautiful voice so racked with pain that when it broke forth from the water, the drops pierced Heilen's skin like shards of glass, causing him to stumble and look into the well. When he did, his eyes met Noelani's. He saw her red hair pooled like blood around her and her pearly white teeth grown long with fury, and he was afraid. And as the jealous are also often cowards, he ran, leaving Stella's body to topple into the well and sink, lost forever.

By the time Stella's corpse had made its way to the bottom of the well, it had turned the blue water black, and along with it, Noelani's heart. Death is a sorrowful thing, but murder is bitter, and crimes of passion are tinged with powerful dark magic that can snuff out even the brightest candle. Noelani's warmth turned cold as stone within her, and the love inside her drowned in a pool of darkness much in the same way that Stella Malley had been drowned in Heilen's.

Still, Noelani had seen the face of the man who'd murdered his bride, and so when he left the naiad's well, a part of her had been forced to go with him, trapped inside his eyes. The love held within Noelani's magic soon soured within him, turning every drop of love he encountered into something vapid and impenetrable until, one night many years later, he drowned in his bed where he slept—as dry and far from the water as he had been able to go to escape what he'd seen that night in the well. Heilen's death was a mystery, for how could a man as dry as a dead leaf choke on water that had risen up his throat from his own insides? But the doctors said he had drowned, and so he had. And because of the curse Heilen had brought upon himself and Noelani, there had been no one left

behind to mourn his death, for he had never again had the chance
for love.

Time has changed the well. What was once a place of love and light
has fallen largely to the ruin of legend. Years have passed since any
girl or young bride or even a widow has dared visit its part of the
forest, for they know there is no love left for the naiad to give. The
well's once clear and flowing water has sunk lower and lower until
all that remains at the bottom is salt from Noelani's tears. The cool
air around the well has iced over, the remnants of Noelani's sobs still
on the air in the form of ice and frost, and the forest has crept in
around the well until the meadow has been overcome completely by
a rambling snarl of thorn and root. The scent of wildflowers has
been overrun by the stench of death, and in the absence of Noelani's
light, the forest had grown thick with loveless creatures both cruel
and vile.

None has seen the naiad Noelani, but those who tell tales of
such things insist that Stella's bitter death consumed the once lovely
creature, her beautiful red hair turned black, and her skin grew
gaunt and pallid like a corpse left too long underwater. Those who
might wander too far into the woods are warned to avoid the wrath
of the well, for even if one were to survive the dangers of the forest,
the creature that would crawl forth from her prison would not be
the naiad, but a miserable and cursed thing. A rusalka they called
Noelani now—a monster, dark and sinister, with a heart consumed
with spiteful evil. And if she saw you, it would not be blessing that
she'd give. Instead, she would pass on her curse and drag you down
into the depths of darkness with her.

The time of the well has passed, and the love of Noelani is lost.
What remained of her magic passed to Heilen, and when he died, it

faded with him—or so those who remember were inclined to believe. Noelani's story has faded largely to legend, and whatever remains of her—whether naiad or rusalka—is left to wallow in her well, guarded by the Court of the Sun and the Moon, who leave Noelani in peace so long as she brings no harm to the residents of Havenwood Falls. Some once whispered of a cure, a return of Noelani's love that could only be brought about from the seeds of her deepest hate, but it has been many years, and none have come forward that might break her curse and heal her broken heart.

And so Noelani waits, trapped in her own darkness, for a star to save her.

Purchase *Of Salt and Stars* where books are sold.